Desert Prince Docs

Doctors, brothers...sheikhs!

When not exercising their expert talents in
A&E, Princes Zahir and Dakan Al Rahal are
renowned throughout their kingdom for their
honour, integrity and dazzling good looks!
Their focus is on their work—until they
encounter two unexpected distractions...

Now, sweet, funny nurse Adele Jenson
and feisty temptress Nira Hathaway
are about to prove to these royal docs
that commanding a kingdom is
easier than conquering their desires!

Find out what happens in:

Zahir & Adele's story
Seduced by the Sheikh Surgeon
by Carol Marinelli

and

Dakan & Nira's story
Challenging the Doctor Sheikh
by Amalie Berlin

Available now!

Dear Reader,

First, I have to say that it was a massive thrill for me to get to work with Carol Marinelli for this duet. I've loved Carol's books for years, and actually the first two Medical Romances I ever read were by Carol Marinelli and Sarah Morgan...so to say that I was excited is the understatement of the year. And Carol was as lovely and amazing to work with as you'd expect her to be!

Despite my excitement, this was one of the harder books to write, and I have to wonder if it's because I'm in the process of reinventing myself—again. I've done this a couple times in my life, and I think of it as the kind of growth of character that makes growing pains worth the effort—even if it makes some things momentarily harder!

My current process is probably why the idea of figuring out who you are and who you want to be is so fascinating to me, and it's a theme I'll probably come back to in future books. Dakan and Nira are each trying to come to grips with who they are, how they got to be that way, and figuring out who they want to be—while falling in love and helping each other along the path.

I hope you enjoy their story, and if you haven't picked up Carol's—*Seduced by the Sheikh Surgeon*—for Zahir and Adele's story, you should. It's really fabulous—not that I'm biased or anything...

Amalie Xx

CHALLENGING THE DOCTOR SHEIKH

BY
AMALIE BERLIN

MILLS
BOON®

HarperCollins
PUBLISHERS
Since 1817

First published in Great Britain 2016
By Mills & Boon, an imprint of HarperCollins*Publishers*
1 London Bridge Street, London, SE1 9GF

Large Print edition 2017

© 2016 Amalie Berlin

ISBN: 978-0-263-06678-4

Our policy is to use papers that are natural, renewable
and recyclable products and made from wood grown
in sustainable forests. The logging and manufacturing
processes conform to the legal environmental
regulations of the country of origin.

Printed and bound in Great Britain
by CPI Antony Rowe, Chippenham, Wiltshire

3475654 ×

Amalie Berlin lives with her family and critters in Southern Ohio, and writes quirky and independent characters for Mills & Boon Medical Romance. She likes to buck expectations with unusual settings and situations, and believes humour can be used powerfully to illuminate truth—especially when juxtaposed against intense emotions. Love is stronger and more satisfying when your partner can make you laugh through times when you don't have the luxury of tears.

Books by Amalie Berlin

Mills & Boon Medical Romance

The Hollywood Hills Clinic
Taming Hollywood's Ultimate Playboy

New York City Docs
Surgeons, Rivals...Lovers

Craving Her Rough Diamond Doc
Uncovering Her Secrets
Return of Dr Irresistible
Breaking Her No-Dating Rule
Falling for Her Reluctant Sheikh

Visit the Author Profile page at millsandboon.co.uk for more titles.

Dedicated to Mr John Bradbury, one of my junior high teachers, for his support and encouragement, and for the awesomeness of having a reading nook with a big comfy lounging pillow in the corner of his classroom.

Also really hoping he doesn't read past the dedication page…the idea of it gives me a wiggins…

Praise for
Amalie Berlin

'*Falling for Her Reluctant Sheikh* by author Amalie Berlin blew my mind away! This story is definitely worth re-reading and fans are in for a medical treat!'

—Goodreads

'Amalie Berlin has proved she's one of the best medical authors of today, and her stories will for ever have a place on my reading shelf!'

—Contemporary Romance Reviews on
Return of Dr Irresistible

'A sexy, sensual, romantic, heartwarming and purely emotional, romantic, bliss-filled read. I very much look forward to this author's next book and being transported to a world of pure romance brilliance!'

—Goodreads on
Craving Her Rough Diamond Doc

CHAPTER ONE

THE HEAT PRINCE DAKAN AL RAHAL had been used to in his youth blistered the back of his neck as he prowled away from the new high-rise apartment building in the heart of his kingdom's capital. Only a few days as ruler-in-residence since the king had flown to England to attend the impromptu wedding of his eldest son, and already Dakan couldn't remember ever having a worse mood.

It also made him aware of just how practical the traditional white robes would've been to wear, not that practicality would change his mind about wearing them. He liked the clean lines of his dark suits, he just liked them better on soggy winter days in England. What he wouldn't give for a brittle autumn wind right now. For just one overcast gray afternoon, he might even be convinced to wear the sword tradition dictated for the ruler in residence.

But until either the King or Dakan's elder brother

Zahir—the true heir—deigned to return to Mam-lakat Almas, he was stuck.

And if he was stuck, the architect Zahir had hired would damned well be stuck too—right in the flat where she was supposed to be working.

Planning the new hospital as part of the over-haul to finally bring their medical system into the twenty-first century was the one bright spot on his calendar for the foreseeable future, made bearable all the bureaucratic nonsense he had put up with every other hour of the day so far. The hospital was the only thing he could get excited about. But the day he'd finally gotten time to come and plan with her, she'd gone sightseeing.

Typical.

Traffic stopped at the light, and Dakan took off, as fast as he could weave through the waiting cars and trucks, counting on the three royal guards be-hind him to keep up. Back on the walkway, his feet ate up the decorative tile expanse separating him from the bazaar blocks away.

At least something had changed since his last time on foot in the capital. The cobblestones were gone. The highly trafficked pedestrian walkways had transitioned to decorative tiles in different shades of sand—something he might've appreciated if he'd only been seeing it in a photo. But here every time his foot touched the walk his frustration increased. Even his fingernails felt tense as he dug them into his palms.

It wasn't just having to fetch the person he'd come to meet that had him wanting to ring one of the jets to go somewhere twenty degrees cooler, it was that he was there at all.

England could be cold in the winter, but at this time of year it was downright pleasant. Additionally, he went where he wanted, never had guards trailing after him, dated whomever struck his fancy, and he drove. He had everything there, most important of all freedom.

Since his residency had ended and he'd earned his license, Dakan had snagged a sweet ride, a flat that made panties hit the floor, and had started shopping around established practices to decide where he'd like to begin the career he'd worked years for. That's what doctors did when their education was finished—opened or joined a practice—but before he'd gotten to see even a single patient he could call his own he'd been summoned home.

All damned fine reasons to wake up irritated.

Another block and the decorative tile walk

opened up to a wide lane lined with stalls on either side, sprawling out from one of the oldest buildings in the city—a holdout built by imported Byzantine craftsman. It had been made entirely too well to do the sensible thing and fall in to make way for a new era, an era that required more than a single clogged lane for people doing their daily shopping like that which faced him now.

It would be just as crowded inside—merchants waited years to get to move into the old building. Even with it practically butting up against the impressive modern towers built in the last decade—luxury dwellings, businesses, and prosperity on display two short blocks away—people still had to crowd through open-air shops to buy their groceries and necessities.

As much as Dakan loved his father, when it came to the way he ruled, the way he kept things always the same—as if it'd been so much better back then—made Dakan want to shake him. Or lead a revolt and then leave Zahir to rule, thus freeing Dakan to return to England.

Just find her and make sure to get her number so he could just call her next time she skipped out as if she was here on a tourist visa. Then maybe make a note to have the clerk write her a stuffy memo about the dossiers of royal contractors out there waiting to take her place should they need to.

What did she even look like?

She was British, so fair probably. Maybe dark hair but pale skin. Look for the tourists.

Scratch that. Look for the guard sent to accompany her. Or ring the guard. By all that was holy, he was losing his mind.

"Figure out who her escort is and call him," he said to his men, leaving them to it and moving into the crowd. He stood taller than most and that helped. It also helped that as people caught sight of him they moved as much as they could to give him room to pass.

But none of these people were the ones he was looking for. A sea of bodies, and none bearing royal colors.

By the time he reached the large arch leading inside, he'd started to sweat.

"They're in the third arcade, Your Highness," said a voice at his shoulder and Dakan nodded, yanking off his dark glasses and stashing them so he could see in the much lower lighting as he picked up the pace.

By the time he'd entered the ancient third arcade, he'd caught sight of the colors he'd been looking for. From there, he looked to the side for the woman.

There was a woman on his left, a simple green scarf covering her head. Was that her? Some tourists and those who worked in the country covered their heads out of deference to their customs...

Whatever, she was British so the same rules didn't apply.

He reached for her elbow to turn her toward him. Wide and startled pale green eyes fixed on him, a boost of the exotic amid the warm tan skin that greeted him. Exotic, but not.

This wasn't her.

He might get away with touching a foreign woman, but he'd never put his hands on a female citizen unbidden. And this woman was definitely a citizen. Damn.

Nira Hathaway stared up at broad shoulders and tousled black hair framing the most startlingly attractive male face she'd ever seen. When she'd zeroed in on his dark brown eyes a weird heaviness had hit her chest and her knees had given the sort of twinge no doubt designed to remind her they could bend in the middle. And that they might do so whether she wanted them to or not.

The man snatched his hand back and bowed, his Arabic flowing like music to her ears. "Forgive me, I thought you were someone else." When he straightened he started to frown and she hadn't even said anything yet.

"It's all right, sir. Though I must ask, who did you think I was?" Her Arabic, though better than it'd been a few weeks ago when she'd really started to pour on the effort, still sounded mechanical and sloppy even to her amateur ear, but it was good enough to muddle by.

Since her arrival in Mamlakat Almas, very few people had spoken to her, the only thing she was actually ready for. She'd been learning Arabic for months because she'd wanted to learn it since childhood, but that didn't mean she spoke to anyone outside of her instructors, who were expecting her to sound somewhat silly. Starting the program as a working adult also meant she didn't give it as much time as she would've liked to. Or hadn't until the last few weeks.

Normally she'd never have asked Mr. Universe for clarification, but he'd thought she was someone else. That meant she looked like someone he'd expected to find, someone who *belonged*.

The dark brown eyes with thick black lashes

she could've been convinced to murder for drifted back to her from her escort, eyes sharpening in focus.

Clearly there was something going on she didn't get. Something other than her having a possible backside doppelganger roaming the city.

"Are you Nira Hathaway?" the beautiful man asked, switching to English.

She nodded and switched too. She wasn't going to flirt with the regrettably handsome man. Flirting would be a dumb idea for a number of reasons, not the least of which being her cluelessness about how it'd be looked upon in this country. Women probably didn't just date in Mamlakat Almas or pick up random men at the market.

"I am. You are…?"

"Dakan Al Rahal," he said, dark brows pinching together to make a slash across his forehead.

Her stomach soured.

As soon as she heard his name, the resemblance to Zahir came into focus. Same height, same jaw, hair color…she should've recognized him. What kind of respectable professional woman became stupid just because a man was…exceedingly handsome?

Though Dakan had a roguish quality to his

appearance that probably instilled this reaction in everyone who saw him. And he was a doctor too, like his brother, that much she knew. Doctor. Prince. Adonis in a superbly cut charcoal suit.

There were probably words he expected her to say now.

Think of words. Any words. English words even.

I'm Nira and I like long walks on the beach and...

Not those words.

"I didn't know we were meeting today, Prince Dakan." There. Words. Should she have said "Your Highness?" That probably was one of the things she should've learned when preparing for the trip, but Zahir had just gone by his name, never once using his title. But here among the magnificent ogival arches and vaulted ceilings? It felt wrong to call this man Dakan, and Mr. Al Rahal wasn't any better than Mr. Universe.

But his collar, with two buttons open, displayed the kind of wide muscled neck that let you know his shoulders and chest would have the same definition... Mr. Universe probably suited him.

"I suppose it was incorrect to expect you'd be waiting there for me to get round to meeting you.

Aren't you on the clock, Ms. Hathaway?" Uncon-
cealed exasperation rang in his tone, even here
among the now unnervingly quiet area of the arcade. It helped clear her fuzzy head. Being falsely
accused was so rarely a turn-on.

"Oh, no. I'm not on the clock. I'd never charge
a client billable hours without working. My firm
only charges billable hours, not days, and only
when someone is actively working on a project.
The first days I was here I organized the workspace and all the equipment, got everything set
up within the system to make sure the backups
happened, but today I ran out of things to do. I've
done some light sketching out of ideas, but—"

"Let's go back to the flat where we can speak
without stopping commerce," he cut in, bidding
Nira to look around them with a simple glance.
Practically everyone in the arcade stood watching them, a sea of wide eyes, alert to the point of
horror. Which explained the quietness.

They might not understand what was being
said—she honestly had no idea how many everyday citizens in Mamlakat Almas would know
enough English to translate this conversation—
but tone was universally understood. She'd angered the Prince. Nothing good ever came from

angering a prince in his own country. Never mind how wrong it felt to be anything even resembling rude or disrespectful. She'd be horrified on her behalf too if she weren't already horrified.

"Of course, yes, I'm sorry. You're right." She gestured for him to go as he wished, shifted her bag of purchases to her other shoulder and fell into step behind him as he wound through the opening crowds.

Some combination of height, shoulders, and *royalty* was what made him imposing. These were his subjects, that's why everyone moved. And he was possibly her employer while the project continued, so that explained why she felt a bit...off now too.

It had nothing to do with the expanse of his shoulders. Besides, no way were they that wide anyway, the suit jacket only made them seem so formidable and square that it added to all the other authority rolling off the man.

They stepped out into the sunshine and the thick scent of spices and incense dispersed with the normal city smells and another low odor she couldn't put her finger on. She'd been smelling it since she'd arrived, something earthy and warm. It wasn't the sea, though she smelled the fresh salt air too. Mamlakat Almas was a coastal city ringed by rugged desert and mountainous terrain. Maybe it was the desert. Did sand have a smell?

She tried to keep her eyes down as they hurried back to her lavish—and temporary—penthouse flat. Not because she didn't want to look around, really there was little Nira wanted more than to look around. And not because she felt intimidated, although having her possible new boss angry with her didn't make her feel like singing.

It was a way of making herself invisible. There was power in eye contact, and this country—as much as she wanted to be here—still felt foreign to her. Being able to blend in was a kind of social invisibility she'd long coveted. The ability to not stand out. She could do that here if she figured out what was socially and culturally expected of her. Blending in wasn't something she'd ever really done at home. She'd always looked different, felt different.

By the time they got inside, Nira had picked up more of the Prince's frustration, but the beautiful interior of the building helped her at least.

Speaking might just help them both. Heavy silences made everything worse.

"I love this building. It's like they plucked the

interior of some glorious old nineteen-twenties New York building and encased it in glass. I expected the flat to carry on the same style, but it's completely modern. Floor-to-ceiling windows, clean, straight lines—gorgeous, but two completely different styles blended together."

Dakan stopped in front of the lift, pressed the button, then folded his arms. In the polished brass on the lift doors she met his reflected gaze and did the only sensible thing she could think of— she continued babbling.

Maybe he just needed more encouragement to break the ice.

"Take this lift door, for example. It's definitely art nouveau." She reached out to trace her fingers along the polished brass design, tracing the flowing curlicues symbolic of peacock feathers, "and I'd say it's actually from the period—not a replica. The way the design is incised into the metal like a patterned window screen."

She looked directly at him again, and her stomach bottomed out once more as if she were in the lift already, all hope that he'd take the hint diminishing.

Nothing but a slight lift of his dark brows came

in response. Was that a sign of interest for her to continue, or some kind of hint for her to shut up?

Probably to shut up.

He checked that the button to summon the lift was still lit.

Definitely to shut up.

Had she really made him so angry by not waiting around, doing nothing, with no idea of when he might swing by? She'd left *once* to go to the bazaar close by, it wasn't like she'd taken a desert trek by camel to skinny-dip at some oasis. And she wasn't on the clock anyway. Her company had no billable code for sitting around, doing nothing.

She should probably shut up.

In a moment.

"I've seen those cut screens in all of the admittedly few places I've been to here. The bedroom in the flat has the eastern wall of windows with these pliable die-cut screens that roll down from the ceiling like you might expect a window blind to do. It makes waking up a pleasure, softens the sunshine into little patches of light to ease you into the brightness of the day."

A bell pinged and the lift doors slid open.

Still no response. And that was top-notch architectural geekery too, completely wasted on this man. Everyone at her firm would've been interested in her description of the building details. In fact, her fellow architect geeks had already flooded her daily social media posts with pictures of the building or skyline, always asking for more detail. Because it was interesting. And beautiful. And unexpected.

He stepped into the lift, and she and her escort followed.

Give it up. He was angry, and that was all there was to it. Once they got up there she was definitely going to be shouted at. She should probably be glad he hadn't deigned to dress her down in public.

She settled in between the men, far enough from each to avoid accidentally touching either, and folded her hands.

Zahir was more personable.

He probably would've liked her architectural geekery too.

The lift stopped and as they exited, the flat door swung open, as if someone was simply standing there, waiting for his return. Probably the kind of deference the Princely One expected, for people to wait around to do things for him.

If she wanted this job—and she really did—

she had probably better figure out how to do that without screaming at him or stabbing him with her 9H pencils. She could sharpen those suckers to a deadly point, and they didn't wear down fast. That made for the potential of lots of stabbing between sharpenings, so very few billable hours would need to be devoted to it. Was there a code for Stabbing the Client? She'd just have to use the handy old 999-MISC.

Dakan strode through the monochrome penthouse, his black suit and shiny shoes perfectly complementing the gunmetal gray tile floors, pale gray walls, and the black and white accents. He stopped when he'd reached the work area she'd spent days rearranging while waiting for him to get there.

Where the heck had Zahir gone?

She trailed to the desk and opened her laptop. Might as well get this over with. She could at least have something to work on and he could leave her to it. Then she could schedule her hours off—one couldn't work twenty-four hours a day—explore the city to satisfy her need to know, and still have a well-filled-in time sheet to show him later with far more than eight hours per day anyway.

"I don't know what instructions Prince Zahir gave—"

"He didn't give me instructions. That's not how we operate," Dakan said finally, as he grabbed a chair from the other side of the desk and joined her where he could best view the laptop.

The laptop and the photo of her parents.

Given the way their meeting had gone so far, providing him a hint she was in the country for more than professional reasons might be a mistake. She discreetly laid the frame down to cover their faces and went on.

"Okay, then I don't know what he told you about how we'd been working. I had done some proposals and pitched other ideas with rough sketches or animations—"

"We're starting over." Dakan cut off her explanation as he settled behind her—which was at least better than him looming over her shoulder.

Starting over. Right. She went about finding and opening the file for the rough animation she'd first thrown together for Zahir and opened it.

"We started by talking time lines and construction methods so he could have some ideas on how long it'd take to have a fully functioning hospital with the different means of construction. There are a couple of ways to do this and I've prepared a sample time line for each."

"I want the shortest time."

Impatient. She fixed her eyes on the screen precisely because she wanted to turn around and speak to him.

"The shortest time line to get full use of the building, of course, would be to build it all and then open it. But there's an alternative, which would allow you to start getting use out of it much sooner but at a limited capacity. Given the current need, it might be worthwhile to have a staged opening."

"Staged?" Dakan said, and in his reflection she saw him shed his jacket and drop it on the table before leaning forward, elbows on knees. "Open different parts at different times?"

"Yes." The animation started to play as she spoke. "In a staged opening you start with one department—and here I started the animation with the original hospital because it's already there. But basically you build one section at a time and finish it for use before moving on to the next part of the facility. That way you can open and just keep tacking on expansions as they become available.

"They do this in smaller communities usually to

make medical care available locally at the earliest possible time and start with, say, doctors' offices. Open those and start seeing patients while they build the next section and maybe add an emergency department. Then testing facilities and outpatient surgery, then open fully with a number of beds and a children's ward, add a proper obstetrics and surgical department, then add more beds. Like that."

Reflected Dakan nodded as he sat back. "I like that idea. Do that. But we don't really have the number of doctors required to staff a building of offices yet. I'd rather start with two different departments at a reduced scale that can be expanded on each side. The biggest part would be the emergency department with some very basic diagnostic equipment—X-ray and a lab—and then have a smaller area to the side where a couple of GPs could have offices in the guise of urgent care for less-than-life-threatening illnesses that still require immediate treatment."

As the conversation and planning started, the tension she'd felt in him drained away. He definitely seemed as eager to get started as Zahir had been, and as he spoke, the irritation that had saturated his voice during the bazaar confrontation earlier ebbed away.

She could work with this man. It'd be different, but he was a doctor too. They had the same goal: get a facility up and running for the people.

"We could do two different reduced-size units. Any time you split your building efforts, construction slows. So unless the extensions are staggered from one side to the other, you're going to slow progress to open new units. Unless you really expand the crew."

"The size of the crew won't be a problem. Will you be designing as we go too? Is that possible? I know it will take a long time to finish a full design, and I'd rather they break ground and get going sooner than later."

Nira gave up looking at his reflection and spun in her chair to face him, her eyes finding his immediately. He was still leaning forward, maybe that was why it suddenly felt so intimate. Even just talking shop, their eyes instantly connected and held just a beat too long for her comfort.

Nira would never call herself shy, but this was all new terrain for her, and she didn't want to make another mistake already. She shifted her gaze to the safety of the middle distance, a thinking point to keep her thoughts on track.

She probably should put off some of her exploring until they got the first unit under way, devote as much time to this as she could now, show Dakan that his goal was her goal. Reflecting well on her firm and gaining a happy client who might ask for her again for later construction efforts would be a great thing for her career.

Her quest could wait.

She could wait.

She'd waited twenty-six years to fill that void, and another few weeks wouldn't kill her.

CHAPTER TWO

"I HADN'T CONSIDERED designing as we go," Nira said. It seemed rude to sit with her back to him when she had no real reason to do so, aside from avoiding looking like a sex-crazed royal fan, which her reaction to him was starting to feel like.

He might be a prince, but he was a prince who had not even responded slightly to her geekery. Being attracted to him—while entirely understandable—would be a really stupid idea to entertain.

Keeping her goals in mind? Much more sensible than some overdeveloped Cinderella story. One-sided attraction should always be ignored, especially when the other side was a freaking prince. Stupid. Understandable, but stupid.

There were other aspects of her heritage to explore without adding "Explore Arabic sensuality" to her list. Besides, Mum had already done that, with disastrous effects.

Focus.

"I suppose I could design in stages to an extent, but I'd need to block out the entire footprint first. You know—the general layout, decide the square footage of each department and the best flow of one department to another before I got started. But otherwise I don't see why we couldn't go in stages with the proper planning. It'll be trickier, but designs are always done with specifications and constraints, so not that much trickier."

And by doing it in stages, she'd actually get to be here for part of the construction! She'd get to see the first building rise that truly came from her ideas. It made the whole job even more exciting for her.

He gestured to a writing tablet lying at her side and Nira slid it over to him with a pen. "Okay, then, you'll start with the split building we talked about. I'll get someone else working on selecting good equipment so you'll have equipment dimensions to work with in your plans."

Nira leaned slightly to get a glimpse of his writing. Not the chicken scratch she'd expected. "Did you take drafting classes?"

"Drafting?" He stopped, an odd lift to his brows. "That's not part of a medical curriculum."

"You write like you've done hours of board lettering."

Silence hung after her words, and suddenly Nira was reminded of the elevator. She'd said something wrong again. It wasn't a stupid question—lots of people took drafting classes in secondary school. Probably. If they wanted to…draw things.

Light crinkles appeared in the corners of his eyes just before he chuckled. "I have no idea what that means. Board lettering sounds like writing on wood." Her shoulders relaxed when he laughed, and a dimple appeared in his left cheek that completely wiped the notion of royalty from his persona.

"It's a way of writing, back to Ye Olde Days of drafting when they tried to make everyone's writing standardized so it would be universally legible. Most computers have a hackneyed font called Draft-something-or-other now approximating the style. I just meant your writing is very neat and uniform. I thought doctors were all scribblers."

"My first education was to write from right to left. When I learned English, it was hard to remember at first, so I learned to take care with my…lettering, was it? I want to be understood."

"Of course. I didn't think about that. I should've,

though. My attempts at writing anything in Arabic have been laughable. I drag my hand in the ink and smear it, or I drag my hand on the pencil and smear it. We won't even talk about calligraphy nibs..." She shrugged and gestured back to the tablet. Stop derailing things. The man might be a doctor when he's not prince-ing, but right now he was her client, and clients deserved not to be interrupted by nervous women trying not to notice how their dimple contrasts delightfully with their square jaw.

"I need to know patient volumes we're designing for. Do you want to start small until you get people used to the idea of the hospital?"

He took the redirection with ease, not commenting on her failure not to smear her practice writing. Thank God.

"No. I want to go big. Big enough it's impossible for people to ignore it. Big and shiny enough to draw attention and bring people in. Starting small just means staying small. It will get the use it needs if we make it important by making it big."

That was a new tactic. Her career experience wasn't yet expansive, but everyone she'd worked with had worked within a budget. But when your client ruled a country, he could probably do whatever he wanted with the budget.

"I still need a target number of patients, because my idea of big and yours might be two different things. And I hate to ask this since I know how fast you want me to get started, but it would really be beneficial to me to see what sort of facilities people are currently using."

He laid the pen down and leaned back in his chair. "You want to go to the hospital? It's barely functional. I'm not sure what you could get from going there besides tetanus. Though, on the upside, as far as hospital infections go, I doubt you could get MRSA."

"I'd like to avoid tetanus, so I won't touch anything. I don't know what MRSA is, so I'll just be glad I can't get it."

"Methicillin-resistant Staphylococcus aureus. It's like staph on steroids, resistant to most antibiotics, really hard to get rid of. But since antibiotics so rarely make it to Mamlakat Almas, anyone who has it would likely have caught it from someone coming into the country. So, probably right before they died, or healed it themselves."

"Right. I'd like to avoid that."

Maybe going to the current treacherous hospital wasn't the best idea. Except...

"But we're leaving the current building and adding on? Blending the old and new?"

That was why Zahir had hired her specifically, even without a CV loaded with practical experience. Also it was why the animation had started with the old building.

Dakan scribbled a few more notes on the pad, then leaned back again. "No. It's on a large piece of land. As we're going to do it staged, we'll leave the old hospital up and functioning—such as it is—and begin construction for the new facility in another area of the property. Maybe right beside it, then tear down the old when the new is up and running."

Definitely not blending the old with the new that way, not that the current hospital was exactly old—it had been built in the twentieth century if the old blueprints were accurate. He was probably exaggerating. Still, she could work with that. And who wouldn't want a shiny new facility? But she had a point about visiting the hospital besides seeing what she was adding to.

"It's nothing to me if the old building is razed after the first unit is completed, but I still need to see the facility or visit a healing center. Zahir—I mean Prince Zahir—said there were a few bigger healing centers within the country. I need to see how the waiting and reception areas function, see what people expect so I can make sure the building feels familiar enough to be welcoming."

He fixed his gaze on her, and for a moment she thought he might finally yell at her, as she'd been expecting him to do in the lobby. But instead he paused for a considered moment and said calmly, "I know blending the old and the new is what you and Zahir discussed, but I really have no interest in that, Miss Hathaway."

With her not knowing what to call him, every time he said her name it made her a little more aware of their different positions. She'd address that first. "Please call me Nira. I don't mind."

"All right, Nira. I've inherited the hospital project, and since I've had a few more days to think about it, I've decided to go a different route from Zahir's old plans. I want a thoroughly modern hospital. None of that modern on the outside and quaint and nostalgic on the inside nonsense either. Modern. Something that would look at home if it was plunked in the middle of London, Sydney, or New York."

"Prince Dakan." She used his title again, since he'd made no overture that she could go without it. "Your brother was quite adamant the king wouldn't accept such a facility any of the times he's presented any plans. He batted back all our proposals already too, before we any got further than conceptuals."

The only reason she had the job was the years of study—or some might say *obsession*—with studying ancient Middle Eastern architecture. She'd only been in the country three days. Prior to that, she'd simply been emailing Zahir proposals, which the King had constantly knocked back. She had loads of ideas, doodles, and even a few sheets of paper with what could almost pass for sketches, but no idea if any of it would work.

"Three days, sitting in a fancy flat in your kingdom, isn't enough to get what I need to design anything properly. All I've seen, aside from a fantastic skyline, has been the bazaar today and the airport the other day."

"My father isn't here," Dakan reminded her, then moved to her drafting table, where he began riffling through the dotted newsprint paper sketches she'd used to think on. "He won't be involved in the design."

"But isn't he coming back?"

"I certainly hope so," he murmured, stopping at the conceptual fountain she was most proud of, and giving it a good look.

"Water makes for a soothing environment. It's good for waiting areas," she explained, trying not to sell the idea too hard. She liked it too much to risk so bold an opening maneuver.

"It's also good at slowing down progress. The objective is to open as soon as possible. Embellishments will come later."

"The footprint, the basic layout, needs to be present for later, though. And there are structural issues—like plumbing and power—that need to be accounted for in the building stage, or you'll just end up having to rip up what we've already built."

"Fine, then put what is required for the fountain in the foundation so it can be added in later. Then put a floor over it and make it useful."

At least he seemed to like it.

"Please don't take offense at this, but I really need to see what is expected now. I don't even know if the waiting rooms can be together, or if they need to be segregated by class or gender or some other classifier. You can thank the internet that last week I learned how to tie a scarf and also that henna is amazing but far too hard for me to do on myself no matter how much I like to draw or doodle. I may know Middle Eastern architecture and art back to ancient times, yes, and I've been learning Arabic for about eighteen months, but pretty much every other aspect of your culture is still very foreign to me. I don't want to mess it up, and waste time and money as I struggle to get it right."

"Aren't your parents immigrants? Or your mother at least?"

Her mother? Maybe hiding the picture wouldn't save her from this discussion.

"My mother is British. Ginger, even," Nira murmured, wariness seeping into her belly. How had they gotten round to this subject? "I know I look like I should know these things, but I grew up in a tiny village in the north of England, where everyone looked like she did, and no one looked like I…like *we* do."

"Your father?"

Her father. Or the mystery that was her father. The wariness turned to lead. "I don't know."

Nira knew exactly three things about her father: what he looked like in the one and only picture she'd ever seen of him, currently face down beside her laptop; that he was from the Middle East somewhere; and that her mother refused to ever answer any questions about him. She had never allowed Nira to explore those aspects of her heritage.

She'd surmised their relationship had ended badly. But she wouldn't be ashamed about it. So what if she didn't know her father? Plenty of people didn't.

Lifting her chin, she made herself look him in the eye. Being illegitimate was probably heavily frowned on here, and he could disapprove all he liked. Whatever nonsense had gone on with her parents had nothing to do with her capabilities.

"My point is I need information or the building will be as culturally clueless as I am. You want people to use the facility when it's open, and so do I. The best way to ensure that is to make them feel at home there."

The Prince nodded too slowly for her to read the meaning behind it, those dark eyes giving no hint of his opinion on her parentage. "We're not so different here. People are still people, Nira. It doesn't matter what they look like, or where they grew up."

So maybe he didn't care? Not that she should care either way, but right now navigating this place required she do a lot of guessing and reading between the lines. But his reaction was far enough from her expectations that she couldn't decide if it could give her any clues for future interactions with other people here.

"They need to feel like they've not been tucked away somewhere and forgotten in a little waiting room, and they need to not feel like they're lost in the crowd of a big waiting room." He grabbed the pad of paper again, thought for a moment and then scribbled down some numbers beside a list of prioritized departments. "Use these numbers to rough out your footprint. I'll get someone working on the equipment, hunt up a firm to handle the interior, and get some examples of facilities I like and want you to aim for. I'll be back in two days."

Two days. Nira nodded mutely. What else could she do?

He picked up his jacket and swung it on as he strode for the door.

She looked at all he'd written down—numbers, departments with arrows linking them up, which she could only interpret as clues as to where to locate them. One department was missing.

She called after him, "What about healers? Will they have their own department?"

"No healers. Doctors!" he answered, not even breaking stride.

Two days later a very tired Nira stood at the massive plotter and sorted out the drawings that had already fallen into the bin.

Any second now Dakan would blow in and she'd find out whether or not he thought she could handle the job, whether her ideas were up to snuff.

She shuffled another print to the drafting table and smoothed it out, trying to uncurl the sheet as the last drawing rolled off the plotter.

"You're still wearing it?" Dakan said from behind her, chuckling as he made his way in.

"Wearing what?"

"The scarf." He nodded to her head. "I figured you'd have abandoned it by now."

Nira reached up and touched the colorful silk carefully. The housekeeper, Tahira, had helped her with her technique in the days since she'd seen him last. "I thought it would be respectful to your ways for me to wear a scarf. And...well, I just want to."

"They're not exactly my ways. My ways are a

little more complicated, and honestly I miss England. Working with a British woman is a perk for me. Aside from that, we're indoors now in your home, out of public view."

"But you're a stranger," Nira countered. Anyone would hear the *Gotcha!* in her tone. She knew that much at least—a scarf should be worn in public or with strangers.

"Am I?" The shock in his voice couldn't be anything but an act, but it still made her smile. "I'll have to do something about that, then. You can get to know me over dinner, and tomorrow you won't have that argument. And then you can tell me why you want to wear the scarf when you're at home."

With their rocky start, she'd assumed that same general tension would permeate all their interactions, but his mood had drastically improved today. He might even be flirting with her—how weird would that be?

"Call me Dakan because we're friends now, at least in private. Right?"

Setting the colorful silk and clips on the side table, she smoothed her hands over her hair to make sure it wasn't sticking up absurdly.

He smiled then, flashing that dastardly little

dimple pitting his left cheek—undoubtedly designed to make her heart stutter.

Good grief, the man was still beautiful, and she'd spent a large part of the last two days trying to convince herself she'd just been fooled by her memory—it was pretty much all she'd been able to talk to herself about. And she'd been terribly convincing. Up to ten minutes ago she'd have sworn he'd only been that handsome in hindsight, and maybe through some kind of Cinderella story memory filter. But here he was, in the flesh, making her insides quiver...

And judging by the twinkle in his eye as he smiled, he was used to knocking women's feet out from under them.

Well, her feet could just get back under her, charming, beautiful man or not. Her goals still mattered, and one of them was not to go to a foreign country and have an ill-advised romance. Those always ended badly, or, if she listened to Mum, sometimes worse than that.

He summoned Tahira, ordered dinner to be prepared, and then turned back to her drawings.

For the next hour they went over the different layouts she'd come up with—high-rises versus sprawling facilities with clusters of smaller buildings and parking structures. And finally settled on a layout that combined the best of both.

"Did you bring the examples you talked about?" she asked, after shuffling off the printouts that had been rejected and leaving his choices on the drafting table. "I'd like to look at them and get started."

"After dinner."

"Or during. We could have a working dinner, look at what you've brought." She looked around him, expecting to see a bundle of prints somewhere. "Where are they?"

Dakan fished a DVD out of his jacket pocket, bumped the button on her laptop and loaded it into the tray. "I don't want a working dinner. But I'll set this up…" His words dried up as he caught sight of the framed photo beside her computer.

Attractive couple. Fair, freckled woman with red hair. Man with dark hair and tanned skin.

He picked it up to examine the photo more closely, and found himself looking at the frame, which was constructed of tiny gray bricks and mortar.

It was very well made, and obviously done by hand—there were just enough irregularities in the bricks to see small fingers had formed and smoothed them. The architect had spent hours constructing it to fit the photo—the one personal item on her desk.

"Are these your parents?" he asked, looking back at her as he did so.

There was wariness in her gaze again, like that he'd seen in her the other day when they'd spoken of her father.

The father she'd claimed to not know.

"I thought you didn't know who your father was?"

"I don't. Not his name or where he's from—aside from a Middle Eastern country. All I have is this one picture."

She carefully extracted the photo from his hand as if he might break it. Or like she'd saved that photo from being destroyed in the past…and now protected it with tiny bricks she'd made herself.

"He looks…" Familiar.

Familiar but grainy—the photo was old enough that he couldn't be certain.

How likely was it for him to know her father anyway? Millions of people lived in "a Middle Eastern country…"

CHAPTER THREE

"HAPPY," DAKAN SAID INSTEAD. "They both look happy. I'm guessing things went downhill after that picture if your mother isn't giving you other information."

"That's my guess as well."

His Big Emotion warning system started to become more insistent. She wouldn't carry around her unidentified father's picture for no reason, but continuing to poke at this situation—when he already knew nothing he could say would make it better for her—was a bad idea.

But the familiarity of the man bugged him.

"Do you know where that was taken?"

"No. She never told me what country she was in. I assume it was his country, but I really don't know. Maybe he was living abroad."

"So she came here somewhere, had a fling, got pregnant, and went home?"

"I guess."

She grew stiffer the longer they spoke about it,

no trace evident of the smile she'd returned earlier when he'd found himself flirting. Instead, her shoulders stretched this way and that as she spoke, trying to dispel tension.

"I'd like to tell you more, but I really don't know anything." She placed the photo back on the desk, though a little further back this time. "I used to ask her all the time, but she'd never answer. And she always shut down any attempts I made to learn about that aspect of my heritage when I was growing up. Burned a book or two, even! One was from the library…"

The housekeeper informed them dinner was ready, and Nira gestured to the guest bathroom. "Would you like to meet in the dining room?" She darted off like someone wanting to escape.

He really shouldn't pry into her background. He liked people. He was good with people. But big, sticky emotions weren't really his thing. Definitely Zahir's territory. He'd know what to say to her to make her feel better—good leaders were like that—but *he* just didn't.

There was one thing he could do very well, which he was pretty sure would make her feel better. Kissing her had been in his mind since he'd dragged her out of the market and marched her back home. Which was weird, and probably some kind of side-effect of being stuck where he usually avoided showing interest in women out of fear his father would start beating the marriage drum again. She might be British, but she looked like those princesses he and Zahir had been threatened with for years. So, exactly opposite from his type.

Dakan went for pretty much anything he could only really get abroad—blond or red hair, pale skin, pale eyes…

She had the eyes. Green and gorgeous, they stood out—not that she wouldn't have otherwise. One thing the scarf always did wonderfully was focus attention on a woman's face. Even without the long silky dark hair she'd been hiding, she was something to look at.

She didn't belong in Mamlakat Almas, and theirs was a progressive kingdom if you ignored the archaic medical system.

When Zahir had rebelled and gone back to England to marry Adele, it'd been because of their father's refusal to change, but somehow their father had given permission for the hospital project to continue as they desired—something he hadn't even mustered the energy to ask about when he'd heard. He was still more than half-certain that whatever work they did on the hospital would be for nothing once the King strapped the sword back on. Another reason he needed Zahir to come home and take over, because if *he* managed to get a system set up that allowed for healers and then left his father to run it? Bad things would happen.

He was probably doing this all wrong anyway, but the project had been passed and even if he wasn't the one born to lead, he had to make an effort. Taking his frustration and questions to Zahir would not only put pressure on his brother to come home and get on with leading before Dakan lost his mind, but it would also upset his brother's newfound marital bliss and further prompt the King to start foisting brides and selection ceremonies onto *him*.

His problems couldn't be fixed any time soon. Nira didn't know how lucky she was with her background, despite feeling the absence of her father's presence in her life. Dakan knew all about feeling trapped. Freedom was important, people often didn't realize just how important it was until they no longer had it. And the only place he had it was in her country.

They both emerged from washing up at the

same time and he waited for her to sit before joining her. "So, how is it you've become an expert in our architecture at your age when your mother burned your books?"

"She ignored the books on art and architecture, or maybe she didn't realize they'd have chapters devoted to Middle Eastern art and architecture. Plus, they were from the library. After she had to replace that one book, she got a lot less fire-happy."

He shouldn't smile at that—really, who burned books these days? But the phrase "fire-happy" tickled him. "That's the contraband you smuggled into your house as a teenager? Art books?"

"What did you smuggle in? Page Threes?"

Flirting. Sexy teasing, he loved sexy teasing, and the innocent look she gave him over her water glass brought an urge to escalate it. "I didn't have to smuggle in anything. I was at an all-boys school. Others smuggled. I just enjoyed the fruits of their labor."

"Lazy."

"Smart," Dakan countered. He could hardly keep from staring at the sexy architect but he forced his mind to focus. Stick with the facts. "Is your mother still living?"

She didn't quite flinch, but a fleeting grimace told him the situation wasn't good, whatever it was.

"She's alive. Healthy. Very unhappy that I'm here."

"Is she ringing you daily and demanding you come home?" He would be.

"We've moved past Official Anger Level. We're now at the Not Speaking stage. I never pressed her too hard for information about my father—she didn't want to talk about him and I knew it hurt her. But I haven't had that same consideration from her. I email her daily so she knows I'm still alive—she has wild theories that I'll be kidnapped and sold into some kind of sex slavery here. She probably thinks... Wait a minute, do you have a harem?" Her voice went up so comically at the end Dakan had to concentrate not to choke on his drink.

"It was disbanded before my mother and father married. One of mother's stipulations to agree to the betrothal."

"Good for her!" Nira relaxed after her near shout hadn't drawn the servants, and settled down again. "But, sorry, no, we don't actually exchange words."

"Are you emailing pictures?"

"There's a thought, but my emails or texts all say 'Still alive.' Probably pretty bratty of me to phrase it that way, but I'm kind of out of words where the situation is concerned."

No matter the snappy way she described it, he could see the situation bothered her immensely. She fidgeted with her cutlery, pushed food around her plate… "Does she know you'd been learning Arabic prior to coming here?"

"She knows now. I didn't tell her at the time."

"More smuggled textbooks?"

Her smile returned, though only at half-strength, and she shook her head. "I only started learning Arabic after I left university, about a year and a half ago. I bought all the units of an immersion language system, but turns out it takes a long time to do a unit. You can't just sit down and become fluent in a weekend."

He switched over to his native tongue, testing her. "So you've learned how to say hello and ask for directions?"

She'd just taken a bite, but paused to listen as he spoke, not even allowing herself to chew before he'd finished speaking. Still at the extreme-attention-paying stage.

Her response was stilted, with many pauses and errors in pronunciation here and there that reminded him of the way children started learning to make certain sounds. They continued at a slow pace, but she mostly answered him in Arabic, with short dips into English when words failed her.

She wanted to explore her heritage, hence enjoying the scarves, and that's what she'd do more of when the project was really going and it wouldn't slow progress.

He felt a twinge of guilt. Time off was important, and no one knew that better than a doctor just finishing residency. "I know most people work about one-third of the day, and I'm asking more of you. You should really take some time to move around. There's probably a gym somewhere in the building—I have no idea. But if not, I can have a machine of your choosing sent up. Sitting is the new cancer."

"Do you just have equipment lying about?" The question went from Arabic to English then back again, but she had a solid enough foundation to leave him confident she'd get better the more she practiced.

"There's a well-stocked gym at the palace. I

can send over whatever you like, then take it back after you're finished with it."

"Elliptical?" English.

He nodded. "Done. And after we get going— after there is a plan in place for the initial building—I'll make sure you get some time off to explore. Perhaps Dubai?"

"Why not here?"

"No reason. Though if you get hurt in Dubai, there are better medical facilities available. Did Zahir have you bring antibiotics with you?"

"No, but he said if I got sick to call him first."

"Call me first."

"Are the healers so bad? It seems like you would have a...low..." Again she paused. Her Arabic wasn't bad, but she'd gotten to the point it wouldn't improve if she didn't force it to with conversation. "Low...number of people...alive...if they did not offer some good?"

"Population." Dakan filled in the word she'd been unable to find. "The healers do some good, but the problem is they often don't realize their limits. My mother's healer realized..." He stopped himself before he really got going. The Queen wouldn't thank him for spreading her business around, but it had somehow started to come out.

"They don't do well with infections, for instance. And anything that requires surgery."

He couldn't explain about his mother's medical condition, or the terrible birth he knew she'd suffered with his younger brother all those years ago, that was all too personal to lay out. Not only for the sake of his mother's privacy but because he hadn't yet forgiven his father for putting her into that position.

The question in her eyes made him want to tell her. He and Zahir had spoken briefly, but as much as he loved his brother Dakan was all too aware that they weren't equals. Always aware of it. Which was a good part of why he wanted to be anywhere but home right now.

"Is she all right now? Your mother?"

The question made him focus and Dakan nodded. "Two months ago she had to go to England to have surgery she should've had ages ago, but couldn't because of the way things are here. After years of quiet illness..."

Absolute sympathy shone in those lovely green eyes. "Is she still there?"

"No. She and my father went away on holiday together. Somewhere. I have no idea where. She's much better now than she had been before. For years. One thing I can say for her healer, he eventually realized the need for surgery, but he's exceptionally progressive compared to other healers. And my father..."

He didn't even really know what to say about that. He probably, in fact, shouldn't say anything about his father, but if anyone would understand family drama it would be this woman, who had spoken so openly about her past. Even now, he saw only concern in her eyes and unasked questions. He wanted to explain.

He switched back to English, not only to aid her understanding but also to make it less likely the housekeeper or any of the guards would understand if they happened to overhear. "The reason I said no healers before is because I don't want them getting in the way. If I give them too much room now that the King has apparently decided he'll give a new hospital a chance, I can see the system being easily corrupted and the doctors pushed into a secondary role once I'm gone and it's all running—which would probably make me put my fist through something." Or borrow weapons from the hall of armaments and do something else violent. "Forgive me. I'm..."

"Passionate about this. I understand. You should

be. Though I don't really understand what healers do. Is it homeopathic remedies?"

"The healers and *attars* work together, diagnosing and brewing tonics and other treatments. But their decoctions have actual measurable amounts of different ingredients—herbs, minerals, food, oils, spices. Most with medicinal qualities. They also try to treat the whole body, not just the particular injured part. Homeopaths focus on distillations of different kinds, taking ingredients down to one part in millions, and largely rely on placebo effect to treat their patients."

"No love for the homeopathic medicine, I see." Her flirting smile returned, and somehow the situation seemed a little less dark suddenly.

"No."

"But treating the whole body sounds like a good thing."

"It's not a bad thing. It's just about them knowing their limits."

She considered his words for a long moment and then tilted her head at him. "So, you want to guard against the King undoing your hard work, but you don't know how they will respond to your decision to change their plans?"

"If Zahir wants healers, he can come back here and handle the hospital project himself."

And, Lord, did he hope Zahir came to the same decision.

Zahir's plan wasn't exactly wrong—it would still be great for their people—but he wasn't only doing things this way to make his brother come home and free Dakan to return to England. Even if that was also a fine reason to do whatever he wanted. Not that he usually needed a reason to do what he wanted.

What he really wanted right now was to make Nira Hathaway smile at him again, something he could do just fine on his own.

"Before you start thinking I'm not up to the task of building this hospital," Dakan said, affecting his most serious frown as he spoke, "I'll have you know I built the biggest Lego playhouse you've never seen when I was growing up. I was a Lego master. Everything I built had perfect right angles and I didn't even try. I didn't even have to use a...a..." The frown cracked when he couldn't think of the right word and used one from her professional vocabulary. "A protractor?"

Though he could see the spark of amusement-tinged exasperation in her eyes—he was, after

all, going to make her work on something that
might very well be overruled when the King returned and found what he'd been getting up to—
she played along. "I don't know, that sounds like a
challenge. Do you still have that playhouse? And
just for future reference, the word you were looking for is a set square. You use a set square to
make things square."

"A set square? Really?"

She nodded.

"Okay, noted for any future Lego house stories.
But, no, I don't still have it," Dakan said, returning to his serious expression. "It got blown up."

Her amusement disappeared just as fast as it had
arrived. "Someone bombed your Lego house?"

He held her wide, startled gaze for several long,
somber heartbeats, and then let himself smile.
"You fell for that so easily, Nira. Not all Middle
Eastern countries are riddled with war and vio-
lence."

A mutinous wrinkle formed on the bridge of
her nose, and she turned her gaze to every item
on the table.

The woman was going to throw something at
him! Food? Something breakable?

She reached for the bread.

"Wait…" The temptation was there to arm himself for a food fight, but that might've been a step too far even for him.

Her hand closed on the still-warm flatbread and she ripped off a chunk.

"Zahir and I stole a trebuchet when I got tired of the little house, made the servants help us move everything to the beach, and obliterated it with a barrage of the biggest rocks we could carry."

There.

A bright, musical peel of laughter erupted from her even as she turned her head and gave him the most dubious sidelong look.

"I'm fairly certain if you look long enough, you can still find Lego blocks on the beach by the palace."

"Okay, you're forgiven for being a dork. And you're lucky you don't have that Lego any more. I might have to challenge you to a Lego battle, which would mess with our hospital timeline."

"Can't have that."

"Would be a tragedy."

"Or we could go for a Lego hospital instead, scrap all this planning nonsense. Cheerful red, blue and yellow bricks. Green roof. Easy snap assembly."

She pretended to consider his suggestion, nodding as she munched on the bread. "I have to ask: where in the world did you find a trebuchet? And how did you steal one, for goodness' sake? How old were you when you got tired of your Lego playhouse, twenty?" Then she did chuck a small bit of bread at him, bouncing it off his chest.

He picked it up and ate the evidence before the housekeeper could catch them. "I was six. Zahir was almost twelve. It was a very small working model from the Hall of Armaments at the palace. One of our ancestors had built this small trebuchet a few centuries back for some reason, I have no idea why. It's perfectly preserved, still in working order, and has since been chained to the floor. We took off with it. Then we both got punished, Zahir more than me because I was six. Big lecture about responsibility and being good leaders, which I've come to believe he took far too seriously."

Talking and laughing with her was enough that Dakan could almost forget where he was and where he had to return to when he left the penthouse.

In the palace and on duty, he had to be serious. He had to be what was expected of him, or at least try to be. He had to be post-trebuchet Zahir, and he sucked at being any version of Zahir—even his crappy knock-off attempt chafed terribly.

Something he couldn't fix right now. It was better to try and fix Nira's problems than his own. And he was starting to think he could. The more he spoke with her, the more he became convinced he'd seen her father somewhere. Not just seen but spoken with. She had mannerisms he'd have sworn were learned but which seemed to have been inherited.

He'd definitely seen that sideways look before. At some point in his life. Here, maybe. Maybe in a neighboring country he'd visited for some reason. It hadn't been in England, and as little time as he'd spent in Mamlakat Almas since going away to school young, it shouldn't be too hard to revisit those short months per year and what he'd gotten up to during holidays.

He'd have to sneak in and get a shot of that photo of her parents when she wasn't looking, so he could have some time to really study it, perhaps jog his memory.

It was in there somewhere, buried, but it would

be cruel to get her hopes up if he couldn't produce the information.

"Now, back to Arabic. You want to become fluent so you must practice. Now, which famous ancient buildings did you reconstruct with your Lego?"

CHAPTER FOUR

THE NEXT DAY Dakan sat in his father's study, signing the daily papers staff brought him, when his mobile rang.

Nira?

He dropped his pen and hurried across the study to where he'd set his mobile phone charging earlier. He'd given her his number in the hope she'd call—not that he wanted her to have trouble with the examples he'd given her, but talking to her was the highlight of his days in residence. He wanted to make her misbehave a little, a desire she already harbored, or she wouldn't have reacted to his flirting in a way that had made him flirt with her even more, a way that made him want to throw off his responsibilities and hers and spend the day just talking. Playing.

Their verbal sparring was the closest thing to play he could remember having had at home since the trebuchet incident.

He lifted the phone and turned to look at the display. Not Nira. But it was the next best thing.

"Zahir. I'm running amok, you really should get back here and stop me."

"Good morning to you too, Dakan." His brother, ever able to recover smoothly from whatever Dakan threw at him. "Have you reinstated the harem?"

"No, but now that you mention it..." he returned to the seat and leaned back "...I like that architect you hired. I think she'd look fantastic in something sheer and dirty."

"It would be Mother you'd have to fear if you tried it. Besides, Nira works for you. Don't go putting your cheesy moves on her."

"Too late." Come on, Zahir, be the responsible one. Dakan hated being the responsible one.

"You're lying."

Dakan tsked. "I'm the ruler in residence so don't start flinging insults. I may have to...figure out some kind of...diplomatic something. Sanction. That's the word. Or sentence you to hard labor. Here. In the palace."

"I thought you liked Nira. It's such a chore, working with her?"

"It's not her, believe me. She's gorgeous and mysterious. And a little bit weird."

"Just like you like them."

Dakan laughed this time. "Yes. Somehow, despite not being my type, she sort of is my type. How's Adele? Missing the palace? Let me talk to her. I bet she'd like to come and visit for a few decades."

"Adele's pregnant."

Dakan's stomach bottomed out from those two simple words. "That was quick."

And that was the wrong reaction...

"Yes." Zahir let the word hang and Dakan didn't even have to ask what it meant.

Zahir wasn't coming home. No way would he let her deliver here, with the medical system being what it was.

"Congratulations." There it was, the right response, even if he had to strain to get it out.

Zahir let the pause extend for a moment, no doubt searching for the right thing to say to Dakan. "It's only forty weeks. Less now, since it's been a few weeks already."

"Right." The filler word squeaked past his lips, just because he needed something to say.

Plans dashed. Would anything be able to shorten his stay now?

"Father and Mother will be back before then. A couple more weeks," the voice said down the line.

But the hospital would still need to be Dakan's job. He couldn't just up and leave as soon as their parents returned, though that was how things had always gone for Zahir: live in London and come home only when he was needed. Hospitals took a long time to build, more than a year. Probably a couple of years. Stuck.

But a birthing center... That he might be able to get done in a few months.

It'd been two days since she'd last seen Dakan, and Nira had spent most of that time working. In between viewing the examples he'd had compiled, she'd spent too much time mentally replaying their dinner and the thrill that had rushed through her with every playful word and flirting smile. But the rest was about proper working, still a lot of work between spells of idiocy.

The only other time away from her workstation was to tend to necessities, so her timecard—not that Dakan had made a single other mention of the thing—was so filled it shouldn't be legal in a civilized society.

Today she'd even showered and put on lounging pajamas to work in. The dresses she'd taken to wearing since she'd arrived were largely comfortable but light in color and they all had sleeves. Sleeves hindered her board work and invariably ended up smudged all around the elbow with fresh graphite—but the pajama top was sleeveless.

Besides, it was just her and Tahira. The guards she had stay outside the flat and downstairs, aside from their hourly checks, so they probably saw her bare arms from the back a time or two when they peeked in and she sat bent over the drafting table, her hair twisted into a sloppy knot on top of her head and secured by pencils.

"Good afternoon."

Dakan's voice rumbled down her spine, and she suddenly wished she'd worn sleeves to hide the wash of goose-bumps racing over her skin.

Thank goodness she'd had the forethought to put on a bra.

Pencil in hand, she turned on her stool and smiled so brightly she hoped it would drown out all other aspects of her appearance.

"Not good?" he corrected. "Well, I'm about to make it more interesting."

She looked at what he carried. Tucked under one arm he had a bundle of blueprints, and in his hand a couple more disks for her. "More examples?"

"Yes. And no. Here, these are all the plans of the hospital that's there now." He didn't say anything about her appearance, but here she stood in the presence of a gorgeous prince, at best disheveled and without a drop of make-up. Her bun felt loose and baggy too, she just knew it was hanging to the side as if she'd had her hair done by a drunken five-year-old.

Lifting one hand, she felt for the pencils and surreptitiously slid them free so she could unwind the still-damp mass of hair. At least that was somewhat concealing, even if it was the sloppiest mess of waves and tangled curls he had probably ever seen. To his credit, although he stopped unrolling the prints and shuffling papers around to look at her, he said nothing.

"Oh, well, that'll be helpful so I can see how it's working now. I just had a footprint of it before."

"That's not why I brought them." He spun her chair, urged her to sit with one hand and then rounded the table to sit opposite her. "We've got a slight change in plans."

"Change? Okay. What kind of change?"

"We're not working on the hospital any more right now."

Nira squinted at the plans he'd unrolled. "But this is the hospital."

"Yes, I mean I want you to stop working on the new hospital designs for the time being. There are bigger worries."

"New project?"

"Old building, new project. So I guess it's still the same project, but we're shifting priorities. We need to remodel the old theater and add a small addition to the building there. The surgical theater there isn't only underused, it's horrifying. I've liaised with the neighboring kingdoms and their hospitals are ready to receive any surgical patients we have for the next couple of months. And when I say remodeled, I mean gutted. Completely redone. And I want a tiny wing added to the side with a nursery to accommodate twins..."

"Who's having a baby?"

"Zahir and his wife."

Nira had to smile at that. She didn't know Zahir was married, but a new baby was always welcome news. "And you want to get the hospital ready for the birth of the new babies."

"It's only one so far as I know, but I'd rather prepare for twins and have it only be one than prepare for one and need incubators and the like for two."

"Got it." She flipped through the prints to find the one for the theater layout. "So, all new everything, plumbing and electrical included?"

"Yes."

"And a small addition with a nice patient room for the mother, a nursery with both beds and incubators, along with storage required for whatever babies would need. I'll need some specs. Bathrooms, and…?" She reached for her pad and made some notes. "How far along is she?"

"Still first trimester. We have some time, but I want it sorted as quickly as possible so they can visit. As soon as you get those designs, I'll hand them over to a contractor and crew for them to get started, and we'll move back to designing the hospital."

A challenge. She liked challenges, but even if her brain still wanted to focus on the hospital, she'd take some time and do this first. He was the boss. Plus, she wanted the baby to be safely born here too.

They discussed further specifications and Nira gave up making notes on her pad and instead plucked up the copy of the blueprint and went to the copier to make something she could write on. "So, am I right in guessing they won't return and relieve you of your obligation to remain here if there's nowhere safe for the baby to be born?"

"You are correct."

"So you're no longer worried about making Zahir come back and do things himself if he wants them a certain way?"

Dakan leaned back in his chair and watched her at the machine, lining up the wide paper and feeding it into the machine. Finally going to address that, it seemed.

"That doesn't change what I want."

"Why not? If you're wanting him to take over, wouldn't you want it to be something we won't have to rip up and start over again? Not that I don't want to stick around here and design for however long I'm needed, but I really don't like wasted efforts. If he's going to just want to rip things up and start over, I'd rather be going in his direction from the start."

"But you work for me, and I don't want to go in his direction. Not only because I want him to come do it himself but because I don't think it's the right way to go. It would be okay, but it leaves too much wiggle room for the system to revert to the old ways. We talked about this."

"I know we did, but it seems a bit…out on a limb with a saw? Have you and Zahir talked about this?"

"Nira. Stop. Don't worry about it. You work for me. I've thought this through."

"I know I work for you, I'm just trying to understand the logic. I like logic, it offsets my more random instincts."

Dakan sighed inwardly. This whole situation was convoluted. She wasn't wrong that this could backfire, or at least get very messy—both his intended direction and his reasons for bucking the direction Zahir had expected him to go. And the feelings stirring within him for the unexpectedly beautiful architect could also lead to something messy. Very messy.

Yes, she worked for him, and as much as he told Zahir he was going to enjoy himself with her, the idea of taking full advantage didn't sit right. Which meant he had to make sure she was on the same page with him. Be temptation. Show *her* what temptation looked like, because he already knew. Those flowing pajamas let him see every curve and every jiggle as she moved around the workspace. They didn't even have to be transparent. Pair them with a skimpier top and she'd be harem-ready.

"I see your point, but even if it chafes you to have to rip up more work at the behest of the Al Rahals, I prefer to overwork you than to provide a substandard corruptible system for my people."

Which probably surprised him more than anything. His first instinct had been to be a massive pain in the butt so Zahir would come back and be the leader. *He* was supposed to just be the follower when in Mamlakat Almas. But those early lessons about duty must have stuck, or maybe duty had become real in medical school when he'd begun to realize the gravity of duty to those you cared for.

"It's okay. I figure you're not used to being questioned. Mild temper tantrums are probably to be expected." She delivered the words so gently and levelly that had it not been for the twinkle he spotted in her eye when she looked at him on her way back to the table with her new copies of the pages he might have wondered if he'd misheard her.

"Temper tantrums are a little louder. This was just me being an arrogant know-it-all. Get it right."

Bending over the table, she began drawing and making notes directly onto the sheet, and her loose hair fell like a curtain, concealing her face from him. Was she smiling? He couldn't tell. Every now and then she'd tuck the locks behind one ear, ask him a question and go back to her notes, but the heavy wavy locks always slipped free of her little ear and fell forward again.

"Why did you take the pencils out of your hair?"

Nira lifted her head and he saw a tiny blush blossom on her cheeks.

"Because it probably looked worse than it does down."

It did. Her hair down made him want to put his hands in it, feel the texture and the weight of it. Made him want to nuzzle in and breathe her scent.

He couldn't say that, so he shrugged. "Kept it out of your eyes, though."

"I'll put it up…"

"No. It's fine with me as it is. I was just talking when I should probably leave and let you work."

"Don't go yet. I have a few more questions."

"Okay." He pulled his phone out and made as if he was checking notes, then wandered around the workstation to where her laptop sat. The photo was there, and she had her back turned. He took advantage of her distraction and snapped a couple of quick shots of the photo, then returned to the drafting table to see what she'd been feverishly working on before he'd arrived to derail her.

Little slips of graph paper had been cut into different-sized rectangles, and each one was labeled with one of the departments he'd requested. She still had one marked "Healers."

He flipped through her sketchbook, looking at what could only be configurations for those departments. "Healers" was always included, but with a dotted line rather than a solid one. She expected him to change his mind, and already planned for it, at least at this stage where it was all boxes doodled on paper.

He'd let her keep on with it for now.

Although she claimed to be a classicist with regard to architecture, some of the concepts she'd doodled were daring and unique, something Dakan always appreciated. He liked buildings that didn't look precisely like buildings. Who needed tall square structures when they could have curves and elegance that stood out from the city while blending in with natural shapes?

"What did you work on for your firm before coming here?"

"Whatever they told me to work on. I didn't lead projects. This is my first time leading. I usually get shuffled into whatever team needs me, and whatever they were working on."

"So how did Zahir find you?"

"He hired my firm, told them what he wanted— as blend of old and new. And they suggested me to him. I interned where I work now, and my supervisor witnessed some of the projects for my last couple of years in university. They all were just that, a blend of different kinds of Arabic architecture. Even some white-walled Moroccan styles. Though I knew that wasn't where I came from, I still like it. I took a holiday in the south of Spain just to visit the Alhambra and soak in its style. It was the closest thing I could get away with before coming here. They still actually have a fair amount of Moorish influence visible throughout the country."

"Moors are a bit different."

"I know, but the styles blend."

"So you really do like this building, you weren't just trying to make me stop scowling at you that first day."

"I really do like this building," she confirmed. "It's unexpected. Do you hate it so much?"

Dakan shrugged and went to sit down again. It was more entertaining to watch her than to look at her doodled boxes. "It is unexpected, and I can see the appeal of the contrast, but it's also misleading. You said you expected the flat to be that old, heavy style, and it wasn't."

"That's true, but I guess I like that mix. Not out of sentimentality either. Although there is a bit of that, I'm not sure how I can have nostalgia for something that happened before I was ever born, but I kind of do. Then again, a lot of architecture affects me that way. I love it. It… I don't know how to explain without sounding crazy."

Dakan watched her small delicate hands move over the paper, sweeping lines and text, feverishly moving until she suddenly stopped dead, stood straighter, and brought the blunt end of the pencil to her mouth and tapped it on her lower lip thoughtfully.

Drawing attention to the soft curve of her lower lip did things to his breathing. Made him need to look somewhere else, but he couldn't bring himself to. Instead, he said, "I'm sure it won't sound crazy. Tell me."

Distract me.

Maybe crazy would take away some of the appeal.

"Don't be so sure," she muttered, but didn't look away from the copy of the print she was marking up.

"Tell me," he repeated, taking a cue from her and chucking a nearby eraser at her.

The bit of white rubber bounced off her hip and she did finally look at him. A sigh and she bent to retrieve it from the floor, sat and focused back on the print.

"I already told you some of it. I had one outlet. I didn't know, well, I *don't* know anything about my family on his side. If I even have a family on his side. Architecture was the one thing I could learn and study that made me feel connected to him. To them. It's a feeling… I can't describe it. I felt it the other day in the bazaar when I first got there, but it sounds strange. Like those people who fall in love with inanimate objects."

Dakan had been expecting some quirky story about inspiration, about building things that lasted. But this was something else. Her voice started to wobble a little just as she stopped talking. Vulnerability.

He leaned forward, not sure whether or not he should ask for clarification.

Vulnerability was Big Emotion territory. And it might interfere with his plan. "You mean..." What was it called? "Objectophilia?"

"Objectophilia? That sounds like a sexual deviant word of some kind. Like necrophilia..."

"It's feelings of love, commitment, and even sexual attraction to objects."

"No. It's not like that." She stopped with another sigh, and though she still looked at the print she worried the pencil between her fingers and tap-tap-tapped the tip in a tight cluster on the print. "The books became like family albums, that's the closest I can describe it. Architecture affects me. I feel something when I see these things with my own eyes now, and I know it sounds weird." She waved a hand, affecting a slight change in her voice as she announced, *"Oh, I feel like this ogival arch is my cousin, and that barrel vault is my sister. Domes... My father is a dome."* She didn't look at him the whole time, and she didn't now, just repeated in a softer voice, "I'm not explaining this well. I know how it sounds. I *hear* how it sounds."

Dakan didn't know what to say to her, but understanding burned down his throat.

He'd thought she'd just wanted to learn, scratch that itch to know where she'd came from. That this was something she'd be able to let go of once she had experienced the region for herself. But it was more than that. This wasn't a whim.

Nira swiveled in her chair and rolled to the laptop to open some program, self-comforting by distraction. Use busyness to distract from emotions.

He could see the wound now. Old, but still raw. And he didn't know how to help her.

She'd been assigning emotion to pictures in books since childhood, probably long before she'd had that photo of her father to shift her emotion to.

Pulling himself from the chair, he stepped up behind hers and began to gather the long damp locks back.

It was an excuse to touch her when all he really wanted to do in that moment was hug her and say whatever would act as some kind of balm. An action he couldn't run with any more than he could his last reaction—the desire to kiss her.

She froze in her seat, her head very still as the long, heavy strands slid through his fingers.

"What are you doing?"

"Putting it back up for you."

Without any direction for him to stop, Dakan slowed down and combed his fingers through her hair, taking his time. A fragrant cloud of her scent mixed with fruity-smelling shampoo, he wanted to bury his face in her hair and breathe. But that would be even more intimate than kissing her. At the slide of her hair through his fingers, cool and sleek, his chest tingled with the imagined weight of the damp locks draped across his bare flesh.

Sweet mercy, he had to just finish the task, get her hair up before he had to tear himself away and make it seem like he was just playing with her hair.

"I don't think you're weird," he said with some effort, though he'd already told Zahir he thought she was a little weird. With the bunch gathered in one hand, he slowly twisted it to wrap around on itself. "It's understandable, you filled a need in whatever way you could." Everyone did things to try and heal themselves. He understood, even if it broke his heart a little.

"I don't know why I even told you all that." She didn't sound as vulnerable then, mostly dismayed and a little breathless.

"I made you tell me. And you probably needed

to say it to someone." He eyed the pencils on the desk. Securing the somewhat neater bun with them was definitely outside his ability. "You're going to have to put the pencils back into it. I've no idea how."

Quietly, she reached up to transfer the bun from his hand to hers in a way that didn't let it unwind, then worked pencils into it in some snaking fashion that somehow held it.

"You say it's not weird, but I bet you don't have any similar eccentricities."

"I'm sure I do. I just can't think of any right now."

"If you did, they'd stand out. There's nothing strange enough if you don't at least lightly question your sanity over it."

One thing stood out, he just didn't want to examine it. Self-awareness was overrated, and definitely more Zahir's territory. His own territory was keeping so busy he didn't have time to become bogged down by things he couldn't change.

He changed the subject.

"Tomorrow we're going to the hospital so you can see what you have to work with."

She spun in the chair and the smile she gave him was a tiny thing but very welcome.

"And I'll make sure you get to see whatever you want to see. You have my word. Domes. Arches. Vaulted ceilings. Mosaics. The royal oasis... Whatever you want."

"After the new project gets going." Nira stood and although she maintained a good centimeter of space between them, she leaned up to press a little kiss to his cheek.

Dakan shoved his hands into his pockets to keep from reaching for her, nodded, and then stepped away to make his exit. "I'll be here to collect you at eight. Wear something sensible and hard to stain."

CHAPTER FIVE

NIRA STOOD AT the wide bank of windows in the penthouse flat, waiting for Dakan in her favorite fashion: while looking out over the city.

Her building wasn't the tallest, though it was close, but the top-floor views let her see almost everything in the city. Without even turning her head, she could see glass towers, squat, ancient brick buildings, and two gorgeous mosques—one built within the last fifty years and another centuries old with a massive white dome.

My father is a dome.

Why had she said that to him? She'd never felt a genuine need to say anything like that to anyone else.

The best architects straddled a line between practicality and imagination, and in the tradition of accepting artists, people usually forgave their eccentricities. Her fascination with everything Persian, Ottoman, and Byzantine had been considered a quirk by nearly everyone she'd met, and she had never expounded further.

But Dakan she'd told the truth, or something like the truth. She'd have told a more accurate truth if she could've defined it better.

Maybe he was right. Maybe she just wanted to tell someone, wanted someone to really understand how it affected her. She had a feeling she couldn't quite name. Not lust. Not some deviant kind of animism—she knew mosaics and arches weren't alive—though she might argue some old buildings seemed to have a soul.

But the emotion was real. Something more than being moved by beauty. A connection she couldn't adequately describe but which comforted her even as it awed her.

Yes, still sounded weird. Even to her.

It was probably good her first official authorized outing would be to a hospital. That couldn't do anything for her nameless woo-woo emotion, surely. But it would get her out of the flat, and on the drive there she'd get to see the city closer but in a way that passed by too quickly for her to become overwhelmed by it. She hoped.

The hospital was a safe outing. Safe. Safe. Safe.

"I said wear something that wouldn't easily stain."

And Dakan had once again snuck in while she stood looking out the window.

"I don't have anything dark colored. When you go to a hot, desert country you wear light colors. So I just went with the most..." she turned back to look at him, and after a glance down her dress found an adjective "...plain. If it stains, at least it's not the prettiest." And she wasn't going out in one of the dresses with graphite elbows and forearms, even if they couldn't be further ruined.

He was dressed in a sharp suit—precisely as he had been every other time she'd seen him.

But there was one strange accessory now.

"Why are you wearing a sword? You said it was icky there, not dangerous."

Dakan made a low disgruntled sound in his throat, "Father's advisors have been demanding I wear the traditional attire—robes and the sword. Zahir always wears it, so why won't I wear it? I got tired of listening to the same comments on repeat daily, so I'm wearing the sword as a compromise."

"Are the robes white or black?"

"White."

"They might be more comfortable."

"Trust me, they're annoying to move about in, though I'll concede they probably have better airflow. It's not that I don't like them for other people, but I feel ridiculous in them. Like some pretender, walking around in Zahir's outgrown clothes and big clown shoes."

She fetched her bag, checked her passport's security, and tried not to look at him. The word *pretender* stuck in her mind, a little clue that everything wasn't right between Dakan and his brother. But pointing it out right now seemed wrong, like taking advantage or poking at a wound. So instead she opted to go the lighter route. "Like you ever wore hand-me-downs in your life. And, just so you know, you stand out regardless of who's around or what you wear."

He escorted her to the door with a light touch to her back, the touch making her all too aware of the size of his hand and the placement of the tip of each finger through the simple cream-colored dress.

Of course she was hyper-aware of him. He stood out—tall, broad, and impossibly handsome, with his nearly black hair a little too long so it looked artfully messy, like he'd been caught in the wind, or more likely some woman had just been running her fingers through it…

It was probably silky and soft too. And she already knew he smelled too good to be real.

He was probably an alien. A beautiful alien with just enough hidden vulnerability to make her question the vow of chastity she'd taken when she'd started down this path to learn about her heritage. Six feet two inches of temptation to repeat Mum's mistakes.

The idea of coming to live in a Middle Eastern country as a woman alone was scarier if she tried to do it with an eye toward dating or romance, another good reason for the vow. But Dakan tempted her to chuck that vow out the window she now stared through to the wall of blurring landscape.

Those sexy smiles… He was probably an amazing kisser. Soft lips, the light scrape of his perpetual three-day beard. Those shoulders.

Fifteen breathless minutes later they got out of the car at the hospital and Nira immediately refocused on the enormity of their problem. The building was small, even though it had been situated on a vast empty lot in the middle of a city where land would not be cheap.

Even from the outside, she could tell she didn't want to be treated there.

"Wow. You know, you look at plans and you think, 'It's probably bigger than I'm imagining it.' But it's actually smaller."

Dakan offered an elbow, and she shifted her notebook to the other hand to take it, and climbed the few steps to the main entrance, only to be left there.

A few moments with the harried receptionist and Dakan returned to fetch her.

"Maintenance is in right now, but no other surgeries today. Feel up to going in while they're working?"

"Sure. Construction doesn't bother me."

"Good."

She followed him across the lobby and down a short hall to the theater.

Dakan warned as he held the door, "They did a procedure in here earlier, so it might be a little less clean than normal."

That stopped her. Nira stood in the doorway, looking about for red. "Why wouldn't they clean it before Maintenance came in?"

"I'm sure they cleaned it up some, but since they'll have to clean it again as soon as he's done, it's possible it didn't get the attention it deserves. If you see anything wet, don't touch it. That's the first thing you learn in medical school: if it's wet, and it's not yours, don't touch it."

"That's descriptive. And…it's not going to be a problem. I'd rather get plaster in my hair and coughing fits from the dust than touch something wet that's not mine."

The inside of the theater was also worse than she'd imagined, but she didn't immediately see anything that screamed viscera to her.

"It's a decent size," she murmured, half to herself, carefully navigating around the table. Once on the other side, she could see a tall ladder set up and a maintenance man up to his waist in an open grid space for dropped ceiling tiles, replacing them. Some fifteen feet up, she'd wager. Very high. Though the dropped aspect of the ceiling would've given them about twelve to thirteen feet at the finished height rather than the ten research specified.

Hearing them speaking, he leaned back on the ladder, far enough to bend double and peer out of the tiles. He said something, but she only made out a couple of words and irritation in his voice. He wanted them gone. But when Dakan answered—

giving his identity and telling the man to carry on—he struggled to right himself back up within the ceiling. The ladder wobbled back and forth a few times, and without a word or another thought Nira darted the few feet over to grab the ladder and steady it.

When it ceased moving he managed to get straightened and back up in there. It was probably not every day a prince came around while he was working, so she could sympathize.

She tried to redirect Dakan's attention, but he'd already focused on her. "Fast thinking. Thank you, I didn't even notice until you were in motion."

"I've seen my share of construction accidents," Nira said, but since everything seemed steady now, she checked the bottom of the ladder for slip guards, and, finding none, let go of the ladder to begin circling the surgery for something to do the job and still carry on the conversation with Dakan. "Thought it'd be smaller given the size of the building, but it's actually okay. I'm going to want to take it down to the wires, and actually I want to take out the wires too. Run new electrical, update the grid and plumbing. Rebuild from the joists up, including a plain painted ceiling. Normally it would be a bit lower than it is—the only ones with this kind of height I've seen in my research have observation galleries, like in teaching hospitals. But here it's just dead space. You might consider adding something."

Not that that was the most important thing she should be telling him right now.

"We'll talk about that later. Right now, I have to say I can't believe they put a drop ceiling in here. Those things give off dust all the time, no matter how new they are. I can't imagine they allow for a sterile environment. They're porous, dusty, and vermin like to nest in them. Replacing them with the same thing is—"

"A very bad idea," he finished, following her gaze up again. "I didn't realize they did that. I've been told that sometimes the surgeons set up an awning over the table, but I thought it was just since the tiles began crumbling—which was why I'd ordered them replaced."

"They're never going to be safe, really, even when they're not crumbling. Bare wires and open joists would be better than those. Also, he really should be working with a partner, for safety's sake. You saw the ladder."

"You're right," Dakan muttered, swearing quietly. "I'm going to leave you to speak to the administrator and start sending surgical patients to our neighbors now rather than during the reconstruction. This isn't going to be a quick repair."

"If he had help it could be done in a day, but there would need to be some intensive cleaning after that, which would probably take longer."

"No, I'm going to shut surgery down until we have a proper theater." The disgust in his voice was impossible to miss. He switched languages, calling up to the man working, "Stop what you're doing and come down."

The man, who'd already looked nervous before, jerked his hands away from the tiles like they'd begun conducting current. When he twisted back to speak to Dakan, the ladder rocked again, but they were both across the room from him.

Coldness hit her gut as she realized the rocking of the ladder had reached the point where it couldn't be righted. The man seemed to feel it at exactly the same second—with one hand holding the ladder, he lashed out with the other and grabbed the rickety frame of the drop ceiling to try and settle himself, but gravity had him. The frame snapped and the ceiling opened above him, tiles breaking and falling as he fell in slow motion. All Nira could do was stare, watching the moment stretch out far enough it would seem she could've gotten to him, but she never could have this time.

Dust kicked up in the theater, but Dakan had started moving. He reached the tiles and bent to fling them back. "Nira, find someone, get a gurney and an emergency team."

"Is he okay?"

"Now!"

She'd spent all that time looking at the prints yesterday and pulled the image to mind. If she went back the way they'd come, it would take longer than if she left the theater and went the other direction, which should lead to the emergency department.

When she'd managed to traverse the debris and exit the theater, she turned left down the corridor and ran until she saw someone in a uniform. Words—maybe not the right words but words that got her message across—came so quickly she'd have felt proud of herself in any other situation. Within two minutes of the man falling, the team Dakan had ordered ran back ahead of her, rolling a gurney and carrying oxygen and a cervical collar.

It would already be crowded in the theater, so she stayed outside in the hallway, trying not to panic, though she still felt trapped and helpless in that eternal second where the man had been falling, wondering if he'd hurt anything vital on the way down and cursing herself for ever letting go of the ladder, or not demanding he come down straight away the first time it had rocked off balance.

Another couple terribly long minutes, and they wheeled him out and back the way she'd gone to find help. There was blood on him and the arm he'd grabbed the ceiling with had a terrible gash on it. What could've cut him?

Once they were out, she got a better view—broken bone stuck out of the wound. The bone cut it, so he must've hit something very hard.

Dakan had his suit jacket off already, but as he walked past her he stopped and pulled off the sword and belt to hand to her. "I need you to hold the sword. It will only get in the way until I'm done. Go back to the lobby and wait for me. I have to see to him." His dark eyes locked to hers and she could see a spark there she didn't normally see. Depth. Something...

She nodded, taking the sword and reaching for his jacket.

"It's bloody," he said, pulling the jacket back from her reach.

So was Dakan's well-tailored shirt. So much for not touching stuff that was wet and not yours.

"Go. Hope he's okay."

He held her gaze a moment longer, nodded, and jogged to catch up.

Once they'd all rounded the corner, and she had nothing else to do but leave and wait, Nira stepped carefully back into the theater and looked up. Ripping the ceiling down was half-done now...though not the way she'd have seen it happen. Above she could see evidence of some kind of infestation, and some mystery conduit she couldn't identify along with wiring haphazardly strewn everywhere. Might've been better before the ceiling had fallen, but now...

Right. Not the time. She stepped carefully back out and went to the lobby to wait, just as she'd promised. The lobby and waiting rooms had been her initial reason for wanting to come to the hospital, before things had gotten switched up and they'd begun planning for a royal birth.

Reception had a desk with an attendant to sign

people in, a triage area, where presumably they spoke to a nurse and went into a queue to be seen, and seating. It was remarkably similar to how hospitals of that era had been designed at home too, outside of those dreadful ceiling tiles that littered the facility.

Thinking about the tiles brought that icy lance of fear back to her middle, and she forced herself to find a seat, then laid the sword protectively across her thighs. Just observe, don't think about that poor man, and learn all she could while Dakan helped him.

Seeing all this live made it easier to understand why he'd been in such a hurry to tear it down, but there were still good bones here, even if the inside had been poorly done when it had been new. It could be remodeled to the point people would never know it was an older building. New insides. Maybe a new facade outside. Repurposing the old, not exactly blending them together, but other than the bones she couldn't see anything worth salvaging here either.

He could die from that wound. Nira knew very little about medicine, but even she knew an open fracture was massively in danger of infection. And Dakan had said they weren't good at treating infection in this country. Closing the surgery probably meant he'd have to go to another hospital with better facilities, which might just save his life.

Nira retrieved her mobile phone and sent her mother a text while she waited for Dakan.

Still alive.

It was in her to say more, but what could she say that wouldn't make this fight they were locked in worse?

I'm just sitting here, hoping a man I saw with a horrific injury doesn't die from infection or blood loss.

I'm doing something good to help these people.

Neither of those would help. There were always other architects who could take her place. She wasn't integral to the completion of this project, she just happened to be the architect under contract for Dakan to use.

She thought a moment and then simply sent:

Love you.

A moment later her phone pinged.

Are you all right? What happened?

The first response. If they could each just give a little, but Nira didn't know how to in this instance. It meant too much to her to be there. And to Mum it meant unfathomable danger to her to be there. Hard to compromise on those kinds of emotions. Just talking would be a start, if she knew somewhere less flammable to begin.

Nothing. I'm okay. Just needed to say it.

Another couple minutes passed, and Nira had started to think that the conversation was over when her phone pinged again.

Love you too. Come home appeared on her screen.

Fight still not over. Neither of them were willing to budge. She didn't need to say that, and she didn't have anything else to say that would offer comfort or clear the air. So she just put her phone back into her pocket and waited for Dakan.

By the time they got the man settled on the helicopter, Dakan could only pray it was in time to save his life. The best they'd been able to do for him had been to clean the wound, dress it, and arrange a lifesaving flight, hoping it was enough to tide him over. Hope and prayer—he sounded like the healers.

Hope and prayer never worked. Any times he'd heard differently, it had always been anecdotal. He'd never seen someone healed because another man had said words over him, had never read it in a chart.

He'd shed his jacket at some point, and now the previously crisp shirt he wore was stained with blood too. He fished his personal items out of the jacket, stuffed them into his trouser pockets and his jacket into the bin for medical waste.

When he'd sent Nira out to wait for him, she'd been as white as the traditional robes he still didn't want to wear. White enough he was faintly surprised to see her still upright when he got to her side forty-five minutes after the situation had started. White enough for him to hope it had wiped that earlier confession from her mind. The woman was too easy to talk to, he should take better care of his words.

"Is he okay? Is he alive?" she asked, standing as he approached and offering the sword back to him.

Well, he didn't want to wear it. Grabbing it by

the scabbard, he tucked it under one arm. The car wasn't far away.

"He was when the helicopter left. And we're past anything that can be done from our end."

"Where is he going?"

"Dubai, since we can do nothing for him here. Their best trauma center has agreed to take our overflow, but the other needed surgeries will be shunted to different hospitals in different countries, decided by urgency and diagnosis. But trauma will always go to Dubai. Let's hope we don't have too much of it."

This ugliness was another thing that made him prefer England. Today there had been very little he could do for the injured man, and that helpless feeling made being home worse. There were always the other aspects, the family stuff—him never saying what he felt, doing what he felt, only what was expected of the younger brother—but this was worse because he should've been able to avoid it. The other stuff he was used to.

He'd long ago accepted he'd never be important to his country, not really. The only thing that could make him so was something he never wanted to see—something happening to Zahir. Freedom to live his life as he saw fit was the only really acceptable exchange in his mind, something he didn't have here. He didn't want to be the eternal follower. Even now, without Zahir or his father in the country, the hospital project was the only place he felt he could make his own decisions, rather than just sticking to the pattern set by others, and that might change at any minute.

"Let's go. I need to get out of this shirt."

His hands were clean, and he took her hand to walk to the car. Propriety be damned. She felt good, and he needed something good right now—something that felt real, and good. Maybe it was just how good it felt to be with someone he could relax around, or simple base attraction.

He led her to the car and got into the back, letting go of her hand so he could start unfastening his shirt, something else he could do around her.

"I wish I could've done that inside the hospital. It should be burned. Everything is practically medical waste here."

Stuffing the shirt under the seat, he tilted his head to catch the gaze of the driver in his rearview mirror, and redirected him. "Palace."

CHAPTER SIX

DAKAN HAD SAID "PALACE."

They were going to the palace.

Nira settled in the back beside him and tried not to look at the extremely nice naked male torso on display beside her. Remember that shirt was soaked with blood—he probably had blood on his skin too if she looked too closely. A good reason not to look.

He was in such a mood she didn't even know if she could even be excited about going to the palace. From a run-down hospital to a freaking palace.

Play it cool. Pretend her stomach didn't swirl with excitement at the prospect.

"We can't stay long. But I can't very well go around the city in bloody clothes, and I don't have anything to change into at your place." He reached over and took her hand again, and the excited swirling in her tummy moved up her torso to collide with the sizzle running up her arm.

When he'd taken her hand to walk to the car, she'd put it down to the idea that he wanted to go quickly and keep track of her. Something besides wanting to touch her. But now...there was nothing to keep track of.

Unable to help herself, she turned to look where their hands joined and up his arm—over the dusting of dark hair on tan skin, over the definition of muscle at the upper arm, to a shoulder she could sink her teeth into. That was the best muscle. She didn't have one really on top of her shoulder, at least nothing noticeable, but that smooth, developed cap of muscle made her keep looking.

Oh, God, she was going to be stupid. He was holding her hand, she was ogling his body...and they were going to what was effectively his place. If she made a pass at this man right now he'd take her to his room. Chamber. Wing. Place where he kept his bed.

Which would mean she...

"Nira?"

She was yanked from the mental acrobatics it took to try and figure out why she shouldn't make a pass at him.

"I'm sorry, what did you say?"

"I asked if you'd mind waiting for an official tour later."

Tour?

"Oh. I... I...don't...ah..."

God. She wiggled her fingers and firmly extracted her hand from his. When she had it safely in her lap again and her eyes forward, it became possible to think.

"I'm fine. Later. I'm fine with another later tour."

It was now possible to think, just not easy yet.

"I mean to say I know we're in a hurry and I should get back to the flat so I can start on the new project." There. Complete sentences and everything. "So, yes, another time."

And while he went to change, she had her sketchbook and her phone so she could maybe get some pictures for later gazing. She could make do with one room. For this visit.

Change the subject.

"You're a proper doctor, right? Done with schooling?"

"I am. Fully licensed. In the UK."

"What kind of doctor are you? You seemed pretty at home in the emergency."

Yes. The emergency. Think about the blood, not about half-naked Dakan...

"I'm not big on emergency. That's Zahir's territory. Initially I trained as a doctor so I could help overhaul the medical system, but then I actually found I liked it. Hospitals aren't my thing. I want to take care of people, have patients I can come to know and keep healthy."

"So you're training to be a GP?"

"Yes."

"You seem like you'd be into something..."

"Flashier? More high profile?"

"I guess I would've thought you'd like that kind of adrenalin-rush medical practice."

The smile in his voice registered, and when she glanced at him, the dimple in his cheek confirmed it.

"Not really. It's valuable, I get that. It's actively saving lives. In big facilities, emergency consultants can often say they saved a life on their shift or maybe several. I just like helping people more than life saving. I like kids and old people. Seeing the same patient year in and year out, watching kids grow up. I like that more. I like knowing I can help someone's life be better. I never get that chance when I'm here. Born to follow, my father said that once. He said Zahir was born to lead, and I was born to follow."

As he spoke, it became impossible for Nira not to look at him. It didn't seem to fit at first, not with what she saw of him. She'd always thought of GPs as more for jumpers and button-downs. When she thought of Dakan as a doctor, in her imaginings he wore scrubs. And she'd never seen him in anything but a suit.

Before she could process this new piece of the Dakan puzzle, before she could even figure out what to say to him, he shook his head. "I don't know why I told you that. I don't even know why I thought it, really. Just thinking about..." He stopped and focused again out his window.

Her gaze followed as the palace came into view.

"You were talking about never getting to help people have a better life here," she prompted, trying to split her attention between Dakan and the palace. What he was saying sounded important to him.

"Right." He nodded, "I guess that's what makes the hospital project special. I'll be able to help all of my countrymen have better lives in one fell swoop so we won't have any days in the future like today."

Nira looked at the hand she'd escaped earlier, and slipped her own back into it.

Dakan turned back to her from the window, smiled, some of the tension in his brow diminishing. "Would you like me to roll down the window so you can see better?"

"I was trying not to geek out and ask. Really, I thought about opening the sun roof and standing up... Your window is probably the more sensible option."

He pressed a button and let it slide down, then tugged her a little closer to him so her view would be less obstructed.

"It's so sparkly..."

"It's Qasr Almas."

Diamond Palace. Palace of Diamonds...

"I know, but photos I looked at online never really did it justice. The camera always caught some sparkle, but compared to this it just looked like some kind of lame photo effect. Click the 'add sparkle' button."

She was supposed to be keeping her cool!

"It's strange, but beautiful. I can't even imagine someone building with that sort of mindset in this century. I'm still surprised any time a new building has a dome, and I love them. You have…" she paused to count and shook her head "…seven domes…"

"Seven is a holy number," he murmured, and then added, "You'll be able to see the large dome from the inside when we get there.

Seven domes.

And a beach that probably still had Lego lost in the sand.

And a magnificent prince who had depth, layers that surprised her, and who couldn't go a single visit without flashing that freaking adorable dimple in his charming left cheek.

"I have no idea when my parents will be returning, but with my luck today, if we stick around more than a few minutes, they'll come strolling in while I'm half-clothed with you, then the lectures will begin."

The car stopped and Nira scrambled out so she could get a close-up look at the exterior stones and the precious stones set into the whole wall. Colored stones—sapphires, emeralds, rubies, and some other stones she couldn't identify. Much fewer diamonds than she'd expected, considering the name.

It sparkled almost as much as the man himself. Her hand still tucked in his, she kept up, not asking a single one of the millions of questions swarming her mind. Let him change and clean up, she'd have time to unleash the barrage on the drive back to her place.

Vaguely aware there were other people there, Nira tried to look the grand entranceway over quickly before they moved on. Minimal attention to people was about all she could manage right now, in the presence of gilded opulence, the high vaulted ceiling of the entryway—a half-dome in its own right—and the carved doors she'd barely gotten a look at.

Alarmed voices dragged her attention back to the living, but it still took her a few seconds to concentrate enough that she could understand what they were saying.

Dakan was shirtless.

Dakan had blood on him.

Dakan held the hand of a strange woman.

Despite the impropriety of pretty much everything surrounding the two of them at the moment, Dakan answered smoothly, first assuring them the blood was not his, and going from there.

She'd forgotten it all in the narrow and extreme focus that had overtaken her the instant she'd

stepped out of the car. She'd even somehow forgotten he was shirtless.

He gestured the people out of the way and began
walking again, and it took her only a heartbeat to
get moving too.

Marble floors, several different minerals visible
along with gold veining that looked... "That gold
veining isn't natural, is it?"

"No. Impressive eye." Dakan stopped as she
stopped, continuing to hold her hand as she bent
over to look more closely at the contrast of pale
pinks intermingled with at least three shades of
sand.

"Why is it there?"

"The marble is beautiful, but fragile. Anywhere
a pre-existing crack or seam opens, it is repaired
with some process that uses gold. An idea pilfered
from the Far East by my great-great-grandfather
as a young man while on a diplomatic visit. It pre-
serves centuries-old marble while increasing the
beauty and interest."

"I've never seen that done before..."

She wanted to lie on the floor with a magnify-
ing glass and study the surface, see how it had
been worked in. With her free hand, she pressed
her fingertips to the seam and ran them along

where the thin golden vein was sealed to the marble. Perfectly level. It felt as smooth, as if cut by modern diamond saws. Could they just melt gold and pour it in there? Marble cracks further with extreme heat...

"Nira?"

"Sorry..." Nira stood back up and they resumed walking. Although the floor had been repaired in an admittedly fascinating manner that was entirely new to her, she wasn't here to see the floors. It was all about the dome.

They walked through another set of doors she'd like to study, and Dakan let go of her hand. "I'll be back in a few minutes."

A meager nod was all she could muster as her eyes tracked upwards.

Not an inch of it didn't shriek color or pattern. The stone walls were carved in high relief, and transitioned to blue and gold tilework laid in a pattern so intricate the only thing her mind could compare it to was a kaleidoscope.

Her vision swam and when the colors blurred together she looked down long enough to swipe at her eyes, but the tightness didn't leave her chest so quickly. She hadn't even looked at the freaking dome yet...

And she'd thought all architecture affected her. The repaired gold marble floors were beautiful— as beautiful as the mosaic—but they had only inspired fascination in her. Not this... There wasn't even a word in her for it.

Love was the word she'd use, but it kind of offended her to think of it that way.

Awe was utterly unequal to the feeling.

Wonder came close.

Reverence came closer.

Connected... Moved...

She finally allowed herself to look up at the dome.

Where the walls started to round into the dome, there sat a short span of stone carved in a band of words circling the base of the dome. Above, the tile resumed, right up to the oculus. So many shades of blue—from the pale light of a morning sky to the darkest blues of twilight—mixed in with shades of sand.

After several minutes, having her head tilted back, the room began to spin. If she didn't right herself soon she'd probably pass out. But she hadn't finished looking.

Not caring if anyone lingered who might notice her strange behavior, Nira moved directly under

the center of the dome and lay down on the floor
on her back for the best view.

Nothing she could've imagined could compare
to it.

And the people who lived there probably never
really even saw it any more. They were probably so used to it that it blended into the background, so they missed how beautiful it was, how
meaningful. Taken for granted, like family—so
at least there was that commonality to make her
feel slightly less sensitive...

She had no idea how long she lay there, anyone
could've come and gone without her knowledge.
Anyone but Dakan. He'd never allow himself to
be ignored for the sake of a pretty ceiling.

Not a sound registered with her as he approached, he was just suddenly in her vision,
standing over her—unattainable perfection with
the curve of beautiful color behind his head.

"It's so beautiful..." she whispered up to him,
glad she'd finally stopped dribbling tears after the
rush of it had finally subsided.

Dakan offered a hand to her, nodding but not
saying anything, helped her to her feet and waited
for her to get her balance.

"I know you think I'm silly."

"I don't."

"Do you even see it?"

"I do see it," he said softly, keeping her hand and leading her from the domed chamber, back the way they'd entered. "I just see as much value in the modern. Today, what happened at the hospital? That kind of thing colors my ability to love the history—especially history not allowed to slip into the past."

Too soon they were back in the car, the soiled shirt now cleared away, and soon the palace stood behind them.

"I hope your perspective changes when the hospital is done. Even if you go back to London. One day, your kids will want to see all this. Trust me." And what he'd said to her about being destined to be a follower, never able to really help his people, came back to her. "We're coming at it from two different sides of the same coin."

"What coin is that?"

"We most want what was kept from us as children." She reached out and took his hand this time. "I want to know all of this, see all this, experience everything that was denied me. You want to do what you feel has been denied you."

He listened—that was something else that made

the man so attractive to her. He listened to everything she said to him. She'd spent so much of her
life having her thoughts silenced, on this matter
at least, but Dakan listened and didn't seem to
judge. Granted, she'd been able to get rid of the
sneaky tears before he'd got back to witness them,
but she'd pretty well bared this weirdness of hers
to him and he hadn't said one single harsh word
about it.

"That's not what I want most right now," Dakan
said, his thumb starting to stroke the side of her
hand from wrist to thumbnail, back and forth in
a slow, thorough caress that sent a shiver up her
arm. Something in the air changed, and the gentle
and somewhat companionable way he'd held her
hand became something that heated her insides
and messed with her breathing.

He pressed a button and a darkened window
slid up between them and the driver, but he never
took his eyes off her.

"What do you want?" She asked the question,
knowing the answer. He wanted the same damned
thing she wanted—to be really, really stupid.

In answer, he released her hand and his arm slid
around her until his long fingers wrapped over

her hip. Supple black leather caressed her body as he slid her to him.

Her throat went instantly dry, and she couldn't think of a single thing to say. She couldn't even figure out whether or not she should kiss the man. This morning, even after the hospital, she'd would've been tempted, but she could've resisted. But something about his unexpected confession moved her. Something about the way he accepted this feeling she couldn't name, didn't comment when it overcame her...moved her.

If she kissed him now, it would be all over. She'd be tearing the man's clothes off the second they were through the door of the flat.

Leaning back, she blinked up at him, eyes wide, shaking her head. "We can't. I can't..."

"You want me to kiss you, Nira."

"I do," she admitted, then followed quickly, "And I don't. I don't want you to kiss me. We can't. I can't."

"You can. No one will see us." The hand on her hip firmed up, curling her in against him even as she tilted her head back.

Oh, he smelled good. And after the cold marble floor at her back he felt even better. Warm. Firm. Strong.

"I can't because I want to. Because it can't go any further and there's something really horrible about this level of chemistry. It's like a trap. And you've been..." Less confessing would be good. Playful. Playful flirting was easier to say no to than this intensity threatening to swallow all her good intentions and every shred of reason. "You're seducing me with your sexy architecture!"

There. That was...well, pretty stupid. Not exactly flirty.

He leaned forward until the tip of his nose touched her cheek, and she could feel his breath fanning her skin. "I thought you said your feelings about architecture weren't sexually deviant."

"It's not..."

"So you mean I'm just here to tempt you like some sexy architecture-owning beast?"

"Yes," she lied. Going along with his interpretation was pretty much all she had going for her right now.

His lips brushed the sensitive strip where jaw blended to chin. Technically, not a kiss. Just some maddening feather-light caress as he spoke.

"You are temptation personified." That was the truth at least. She turned her head so they were nose to nose, before he actually kissed her neck or her ear in some dastardly sexy checkmate. That'd be worse than kissing her lips.

"Because you want to be a good girl," he said, his voice still low, a deep throaty timbre that summoned an ache low in her belly, his lips barely touching hers as he spoke. "You turned your mouth to mine. Does that mean you want me to kiss you now, *ya amar*?"

Ya amar. Speaking Arabic to her when she could barely think in English.

"No." *Yes.*

Her heart hammered in her chest, but she balled her hands into fists so they wouldn't do anything impetuous, like reach for him.

His words finally translated in the fog of her mind and she asked, "Like the moon?"

"Beautiful." He whispered the explanation, stroking her ego in one word, but calling her on her lie with his next words. "You want me to kiss you despite all your denials. Take the choice away."

And it was a strike against her willpower and her devotion to the rights of women that he was right.

Her stay in Mamlakat Almas was supposed to

be a guidepost to help her figure herself out, in order to explore what she might've been had she been raised here. Even counting out the track record Hathaway women had with Middle Eastern men, she shouldn't sleep with him—embracing what she might've been meant wrestling with the idea of chastity. Even if it was a little late for that, technically. She couldn't go abandoning her admittedly possibly temporary principles over pure lust.

But in the back of her mind, if he kissed her, as the instigator, he absolved her from blame. Like that was even minutely acceptable!

Whoops, went to a foreign country and the sexiest prince in existence ravished me in the back of a limo. Rascally Prince. What can you do?

"That's unfortunate," he said, letting go of her abruptly as he drew back. "Because I'm not going to do that. I'm not going to kiss you until you're begging for it." The car rolled to a stop and she realized only when he opened the door and got out that they'd arrived. Her workspace waited for her.

On quivering legs, she managed to crawl out behind him and stand, but Dakan blocked her in against the car, holding the door with one hand as the other went to her hip. Still with that low seductive purr, he whispered at her ear.

"And you will beg me for it, *habibi*. Because you're not going to be able to think of anything but the way my mouth would feel on yours, on your skin, at your breast. You want me as much as I want you. The sooner you come around to admitting it, the happier we'll both be."

He squeezed her hip and let go of her, stepping back so that the door was clear.

She searched for something to say—anything to say—but came up blank. A girl could fantasize her whole life about someone throwing down such a sexy gauntlet, and in every fantasy she'd have a saucy comeback.

Nira had no saucy comeback.

All she managed to do was nod, and mutter, "Okay."

Walking took almost as much concentration, and she was glad he got back into the car and it pulled away so he wouldn't see her wobbling her way into the building.

Him leaving was probably all that saved her from begging right then.

CHAPTER SEVEN

FOR THE NEXT WEEK, Nira didn't see Dakan once. He phoned every couple of days to check she didn't need anything, letting her work and stew in her own confusion.

Or maybe it was some other reason. Maybe he'd thought better of his sexy gauntlet. That would be a good reason to stay away. It's not like there weren't a billion women in the world who would love to pick up his sexy gauntlet. But she might very well be the only one within driving distance, unless he was looking for a wife, and something told her he wasn't.

The only part of her mind able to achieve any kind of clarity was the part that got absorbed in the work. And that had been sadly waning since she'd shipped the theater plans off to her firm to check a couple of days ago.

Now, while waiting, she alternated between working on the wing addition and re-re-re-checking the changes she'd made. Remodels were always harder to work out than fresh builds and she didn't want something to slip through.

Equipment specs she'd been given all fit within the new footprint in a workable order, so was wheeled equipment that could be moved to the table.

The new electrical grid gave extra room for demands that might arise in the future, and had been double-checked before she'd sent the plans in for approval.

Dakan probably wouldn't mind her knocking out a wall to make the theater include a small scrub bay that should've always been there. But who knew what Dakan was thinking? She'd had him pegged for a sexy charmer used to getting his way, but that confession... It didn't seem like he got his way much here.

These alternating opinions were going to make her seasick.

Her email pinged with the plans being sent back to her. Nira opened to check for notes and, finding none, reached for her phone.

Nira had not once called Dakan yet. She'd worked as much as possible because during the moments when her mind became quiet she had a hard time ignoring his prediction. If that's why he'd stayed away, it was dastardly cunning.

She'd never begged for a kiss in her life—let alone for sex—but the pendulum of her opinion swung between certainty all would be well if she did exactly what he said, and certainty she'd end up way over her head. The shadow of her birth and the ghost of her mother's heartache had left a mark on her.

Mum hurt twenty-seven years later. The love she'd felt had twisted into something closer to hate, but that pain never went away.

Nira couldn't even predict how she might react in her mother's shoes, only that if she fell for him it'd mean heartache. This was a culture of arranged marriages, and she was no one. She had no auspicious background or elite family history. She didn't even really understand the culture beyond snapshots, generalizations, and probably the occasional accidental stereotype.

This wasn't going to get her anywhere. She wasn't looking for a husband right now anyway. She had yet to meet New Future Nira—whoever she'd be when she filled in the missing pieces—before she could even think about her future.

Just call him, already. If it's for work it doesn't count.

She dialed.

A moment later, he answered, *"Hal tashtaaqo lii?"* *Do you miss me?*

Yes, she bloody well did miss him. More than that, the sound of his voice sent a thrill through her that could only be fueled by the probability she was about to make a very stupid decision.

"I have approved plans ready for the theater. Do you want me to print them out and make copies for your contractor?"

"What about the royal wing addition?" He flowed with the way she steered the conversation, though a hint of amusement hung in his tone.

"Not done yet, but it's coming along. I expect to have new plans ready to send to home for review by the end of the week."

"So in three or four days?"

"I hope to send it on Friday so it can be reviewed on Monday and Tuesday in the respective meetings," she answered, then leaned back in her chair, chewing her lower lip. "So do you want the prints?"

"Yes," he answered. "Why don't you get them ready and I'll come for dinner?"

No. Say no. Fake a headache.

No. He'd want to diagnose that.

Tell him she was going to bed early.

God, no, don't bring up beds.

But hadn't she just been thinking about how he never got his way in things?

Keeping her tone light, so it didn't sound like a rejection, Nira said, "You may be the ruler-in-residence, but I think I'm still the one who is supposed to invite you over."

"You wish to invite me over? Very well! I graciously accept. I'll even bring dinner if you don't want to tax the housekeeper with a last-minute dinner."

Maybe he did get his way sometimes, probably by doing exactly this. Because it worked. He made it hard to say no to him. Not just his stubbornness, but he made her not want to say no to him. Made it hard not to want to play this ill-advised game.

"Her name is Tahira, and she's actually already cooking and always makes way more than I can eat. So, yes, you may come over."

For once, Dakan knocked.

Nira heard the rap on the door and it took her a moment to realize what it was. He never knocked.

She called, so Tahira didn't go scrambling for the door, "I'll get it."

When she opened the door, he was smiling, "Oh, wearing trousers. Scandalous," he said, winking as he slipped around her and waited for her to close the door. He'd ditched his usual suit for once and the flowing linen tunic and trousers looked even better on the man. So unfair. The clean whiteness made his usual scruff that much darker, and set off the polished bronze of his skin. The fact that he looked so happy probably also added to his aura of beauty.

Obviously he hadn't suffered a moment of doubt or confusion for the past week. He'd probably slept like a baby every night.

"You're in a very good mood."

"Of course I am. I'm here to get plans that will facilitate me returning to my life, and also? I believe I'm getting kissed."

Nira's heart gave a little flip when he said "kissed." "I didn't say that."

He offered his elbow, and she stared at it a beat too long before slipping her hand through it.

"We can talk about that later. For now, I have some news I thought you'd be interested in. Want the good news first, or the really good news?"

Bypassing the desk and seating, Dakan guided her to the stunning floor-to-ceiling windows. The early evening sky had started to change color; soon the sun would be going down, and all the windows in the city reflected a hazy shade of rose.

"The good news, I guess."

"I just came from the hospital. The man we sent to Dubai? He's home. He got back today and I went to see him and what they sent back. He's doing very well."

That might explain the lightness in his step, attire, and demeanor. "That's wonderful news. You sure that's not the really good news?"

"I don't know. I lied, I couldn't decide which was better so I prioritized the one that'll make your life easiest and most interesting."

"Okay. Let me have it," Nira said. "Unless it's that you've found a more experienced hospital designer. Don't think I want to hear that even if it'd make my life easier and more interesting."

"Your job's safe. For now," he said, dragging her in front of him so she stood sandwiched between his firm heat and inches from the hard, bright window.

The instant she felt his chest against her back, the decision was made. She was going to kiss him, at the very least. Something else might happen but, smug or not of him to think so, he was right.

His hands slipped onto her hips and then around her waist to link loosely at her belly. Yes. Definitely completely at ease with the situation.

Would he have even a drop of hesitation about this? If she could get a peek at his pros and cons list about kissing her—or sleeping with her—would there even be anything in the cons column?

"You were right about the hospital. It looks like the royal wing will be finished in time for the baby, and the operating theater remodeled. It'd be foolish of me to continue going down a different road from the one Zahir and my father agreed on if I still plan on handing it back later. And, look, I've come to the conclusion before you got back to working on those plans."

"That's good news," Nira murmured, but her thoughts or interest just weren't on the hospital. Meeting his gaze in the reflection on the window, the need to know took over her mouth. "Do you have any reservations about this? About something happening with us? I don't even know what's going to happen and I'm very conflicted, but you just don't seem to—"

He stopped her by sliding his hands back to

her hips and stepping back enough to turn her to face him.

"Of course I have reservations," he said, brows drawing together above those deep brown eyes. "Not about whether I'd enjoy it, not about whether you would either. But one reservation is the possibility we'll get too involved in bed. I only get a few hours a week to come here as it is, and if we spent all those hours in bed, that'd be detrimental to the project."

It made her feel better to know he had doubts. Doubts fueled her nearly twenty-four hours a day, so absolute confidence worried her.

"What else?"

"That you'll forget where I stand and get hurt like your mother was hurt. Not pregnant, but just hurt. You don't have anyone but me in Mamlakat Almas."

"I don't really know where you stand, so that's a valid worry." She stepped to the side, as facing him in that narrow space between him and the windows was too much. "Never mind, this is too weird. Let's just have a nice dinner and not worry about that."

"No."

She'd stepped past him when he stopped her by

catching her wrist, and once more sensation radiated from where he touched her. These kinds of reactions were the problem. Couldn't they make some kind of pill to turn that off?

"If you don't know where I stand, that needs to be remedied. I'll be clear. I like you. I think you're funny and clever, I think you're kind of strange in your devotion to living a lifestyle you have no idea how to live, but it makes you interesting. I also think you're beautiful and sexy, and before long I'll be gone from here, but you'll still be here, working with my brother."

"So, where you stand is…you like hanging around with me while you're here, but after you're gone, that's it."

For the first time since he'd arrived, Dakan frowned, but he didn't deny it. He nodded even as his thumb once more began that maddening stroking over her skin, though it wasn't an unconscious thing. She recognized it now as an attempt at comfort. He knew how it sounded, he knew it sat wrong with her, and wanted to make it all right.

"I doubt your mother was afforded that level of clarity. The kind of heartbreak you spoke of—that could only come from being blindsided and feeling betrayed. I can't betray you if you know at the start I'm going to be gone in a couple of months."

"Okay. I know where you stand now."

She already knew that, but maybe he already felt important to her because she was so isolated here. She needed to make some friends not obligated to be nice to her to protect their livelihood.

His words came back to her then and she tilted her head to look up at him. "Is this why my life is going to be more interesting?"

He let go of her hand, allowing her to put a little more space between them. Her arms felt shaky, so did her knees. She still wanted to kiss him. Okay, one more step back...

"We're going to visit a few healing facilities in the country. I'm hesitant to call them facilities or centers. That makes it sound more organized than it is. But there are places with healers and different sorts of healing baths and treatments. They are like a strange mix of a spa and a doctor's office."

"We're going to go together? I get to go?"

"You get to go. I need you to see what they do so we can try and replicate some of it here."

She felt the smile blooming from her belly before it ever reached her face. Somewhere outside the city, somewhere she'd probably find a more authentic location to what she would've had had her parents not split up—something more everyday than penthouses and palaces studded with precious stones.

If she hadn't wanted to kiss him before... Her gaze drifted to his mouth.

One of them had to go before she threw herself at him.

Staying away for a week had been hard. Dakan's mood had been so black prior to today that Bashir—his father's aide—had constantly sent the *attar* to him to try and get him to drink a potion to help. It wasn't until today and hearing his first official patient was returning that he'd found something to smile about. Nira's call had come right when it could make the day good enough to wash away the previous seven.

He still needed to kiss her and wasn't keen to examine why just yet. The way she looked at his mouth made the perfect excuse to forget his challenge.

He leaned down to her ear and whispered, "Kiss me, woman, or make a liar of me. I'm pretty damned sure I don't care any more if you beg or not, just kiss me."

The breath that stuttered out of her open mouth sounded like a plea and then like a lament.

"I can't." She shook her head, stepping away, pausing to judge the distance between them, and then moving another meter away. "I'm not going to sleep with you. I can't do that and then travel around the country with you. Everyone would be able to look at me and see we were lovers. I want to kiss you. I want more than to kiss you, but… could you stop with a kiss tonight?"

Could he stop at one kiss?

Dakan watched her chest rise and fall far too rapidly for anything but excitement, fear, or both—considering the situation.

His mind was made up before he started moving, "Let's find out."

Three short strides and he reached her. She didn't move away again; she didn't ask for more assurances or answers. His hand slid into her hair to cradle her head and he pulled her to him.

His lips touched hers and the fire that had been threatening to eat through his will exploded in his belly, met by an equal hunger in her kiss. She slid her arms free of his waist to wrap them around his shoulders, leaning into him as she held him curled down to meet her, pressing every inch of her body against him that she could.

Her mouth opened and Dakan took the invitation to take the kiss as deep as he'd been dying to since that first day he'd met her.

It wasn't enough.

He wanted greater contact, to mash himself against her the way her whole body invited him to.

When his lungs began demanding air he still wasn't ready to stop. Breaking from the sweet mouth that held him captive, he trailed kisses across her cheek and down the side of her neck, letting his hands roam her body to settle beneath the cheeks of the plump swell of flesh that had jiggled so temptingly at him when he'd caught her working in her pajamas. He squeezed, pulling her hips against his.

A stuttering breath and a groan preceded the softly whispered, "Stop. We have to stop..."

He stopped kissing, but didn't release her yet.

The urge was there to convince her otherwise, but she said to stop.

Reluctantly, he let go of her bottom and moved away. The linen trousers, which had seemed so comfortable and casual, now might as well be a spotlight to the effect she had on him.

"I'm sorry," she said, but made a point of not looking down. "I just can't."

"So you said." Another deep breath and he got his pulse slowed down, then broke away to head for her desk area. She had plans for him, he'd get those at least before leaving.

"Do you want to stay for dinner?"

It was the apology he still heard in her voice that helped his frustration subside somewhat, that and the breathless quality that at least confirmed that she was as affected as he was. "No. I'll take the plans and go home. Let me know about the private wing, and I'll call you with our itinerary at the end of the week."

If he went straight home and into a cold shower, he might be ready to travel by next week. Or he might be wearing the robes for other reasons.

CHAPTER EIGHT

"TAKE THE LUGGAGE to my suite, along with the packages." The voice of Dakan's mother rang out from the front entrance, bright and happy.

They were home.

Dakan stood immediately and went to greet his parents. Or just his mother. The King was nowhere to be seen. "Welcome home, Mother. Did you have a good holiday?"

Ever the loving and affectionate parent, she hugged him hard and kissed both of his cheeks. "I had a wonderful holiday. Have you heard from Zahir? How is Adele?"

"Pregnant," Dakan answered, keeping an arm around his mother's shoulders as he steered her toward a settee.

"Yes, isn't it wonderful?"

"It is." For them. And it would be for his parents and the kingdom as well, just as soon as Dakan got the facilities up to date.

"Is the architect working on the hospital?"

Dakan stopped a moment and then nodded. "We've had to take small pause with that, but she's already gotten together plans for the surgery theater to be remodeled and modernized, and she's finalizing plans for a small wing off that short side of the hospital for family. It will be tight, but the contractor assures me that it's small enough to have finished by the time Adele delivers. After the plans are approved by her firm, the architect and I are taking a small trip around the kingdom to different healing centers to see how it can be incorporated into the hospital planning."

"Oh, that's wonderful. You've been busy."

Staff arrived and summoned them to a late lunch, and over the next hour he listened to his mother gush about the vacation and the different countries they'd visited.

Tabda Aljann.

The man in Nira's picture swam to the front of his mind along with the sudden certainty that he'd seen the man in Tabda Aljann as a child. One of the Al-Haaken family. Jibril? Maybe.

"Dakan?"

He forced himself to focus on his mother. "Forgive me, Mother. I got…a little distracted."

"Are you feeling all right? The color drained right out of your face. Should I send for the *attar*?"

"I don't need any tonics. I just remembered something." He fumbled for his phone and then flipped through until he found the photo of Nira's parents. Maybe it wasn't him. Mother had probably recently dined with the whole family, so if she knew him—and she'd known that family since she'd turned down their king's marriage proposal and married Dakan's father instead—she'd have seen him.

Damn. Showing his mother the photo might backfire on him and take the Nira situation out of his hands, but his memory wasn't good enough to proceed alone.

"Mother, do you recognize this man?" He handed the phone to her. "I know it's not the best quality."

"Oh, yes, this is Prince Jibril. We had dinner with his family when the yacht put in at one of their ports on our cruise. Who is this woman with him?"

Dakan eased the phone back and turned it off. He didn't want to lie to her, but he also didn't want to tell her that the architect was blood kin to the royals in a nearby country. Especially when he knew that dinner his parents had attended would've been tense already—things had never been what anyone sane would call friendly since that denied proposal, though they made a show of pretending they were.

"I don't know her name," he admitted.

"Where did you get the photo?"

"A friend." His mother would probably have better advice on how to handle this than anyone else in his family. At least she'd be sympathetic with Nira. Slowly, and minimizing the detail as much as he could, he told his mother the scant story of Nira's birth.

"She'll be very happy when you tell her you've found him."

"I don't know if I'm going to tell her."

"Why not?"

"Because she wants to know so badly she might hop on a jet, march up to the palace and demand to know if he's her father."

"You're afraid she might leave? Or that she might get hurt?"

"Both. She's got a good head for design, works fast and hard. Zahir did well in hiring her. But I've come to know her since she's been here and she could be very easily hurt if he responded in any way other than joy at seeing her. Something tells me he wouldn't be happy to see her, and neither would King Ahmad. Jibril's married, isn't he?"

"For a long time," Leila confirmed, then a little more slowly asked, "How old is she?"

"I don't know. Maybe a few years younger than me."

"His eldest son is Zahir's age."

He rubbed his head, an ache stabbing behind one eye suddenly. "I can't tell her. Not yet. Maybe in a while."

"Dakan, if she's of royal blood, even if she is illegitimate we can't have her living alone and going about alone in the city. It's just not acceptable."

"She's not living entirely alone. She's got a live-in housekeeper and Zahir put guards on her to serve as her escorts."

"But she's still alone. She doesn't have anyone to look out for her well-being."

"She has me," Dakan said, then immediately regretted it as his mother's brows shot skyward. "She's my friend. I'll keep anything bad from happening to her."

"You know that's not proper. Your father will insist."

"Then don't tell him. We're going to go visiting some healing centers next week—that will give me some time to ease her into the whole thing."

"I won't lie to him."

"You don't have to lie. You just have to not mention it for a week or so."

He didn't want Nira living at the palace, and that's exactly what would happen the instant his father heard about this. He needed her in the penthouse, away from here. Somewhere they could be alone, yes, but not just because he lusted after her as if he'd never had a woman in his life. He needed to be alone with her, just talking with her and relaxing. She'd become his sanctuary, his Little London.

"You care for her."

He tried to think of what he could say to explain. His family loved him and he them, but he never truly felt understood when he was home. Which probably had something to do with his difficulty understanding himself sometimes. But Nira seemed to get him. Where words failed him, he simply nodded. "Yes. But don't go getting ideas."

"Who? Me? I have no ideas whatsoever. I'm

sure the last idea I had was…in the nineties. And I'm far too tired to have ideas right now." She stood, bent and kissed the top of his head, and then wandered out of the room. "I think I'll have a nap. Then I need to get back to planning the party for Zahir and Adele, see where arrangements have been left. But first I'll send the *attar* to you with a tonic for your head."

"Why?"

"It's hurting. You always rub your forehead like that when your head hurts."

Maybe she did understand him better than he gave her credit for. She knew that much, at least. "Thank you, Mother. I'm glad you're home."

"Me too," she called, already out of the room.

The tour wouldn't take more than a few days, certainly not the whole week. He had until the last day at the latest to figure out how to tell Nira what he'd learned.

How did you tell someone they were very likely a royal bastard?

Nira dressed for practicality on the first day of their tour in loose-fitting linen trousers, a long tunic to cover her neck to wrists, and a matching scarf. The scarf still felt important to her. She wanted to belong, or at least feel like she could. Dressing correctly was an easy start, something she could control. And maybe people would see that she was trying, and give her a little more leeway if she did mess up or cause accidental offense. Kind of like an advance apology.

She heard the key in the lock and stood, grabbing the bag she'd packed with her sketchpad and pencils. They, together with her fully charged phone, would allow her to document anything she needed with sketches and or photos.

"Good morning," she said, her voice a little too chipper, but it morphed into surprise. Dakan wore robes, head to toe, he was like some exotic vision of a sexy lord of the desert.

He'd refused the robes every single other time she'd seen him, but now he was going to wear them? Even the brooding expression he wore couldn't detract from the effect he was having on her pulse.

"Did your advisors knock you down and change your clothes?"

"I'd actually even take that scenario." He placed two bags on the floor—one large canvas duffle bag and a suitcase. His hands free, he gathered up the yards of material of his robes, lifted them to show her the simple white linen trousers and T-shirt he wore beneath. "My parents returned from their holiday. The King insisted I wear robes since we're going out into the countryside in an official capacity. I'm stuck in them for the duration of the trip—which will actually be a little longer now."

"Why is that?"

"Tomorrow Father is sending me to the Immortal Fortress," Dakan answered. "Us, rather. I'll need entertainment, and I suppose this fits in with your desire to explore the culture. So you'll just be stuck with me for an extra day and we'll resume our trip on Wednesday and Thursday."

"What's the Immortal Fortress?"

"You don't know the story?"

"It's not one I'm familiar with."

"It's a fortress in the desert near the border. Very old, functionally abandoned until the yearly race. Traditionally, it's the King's duty, but since we were going to be out of the capital tomorrow, if he also goes into the desert, there are no Al Rahals within easy reach. There must always be a ruler in residence within easy reach. I'll tell you all about it tomorrow. We'll go and watch the race, crown the winner, and get back here for a relaxing evening."

A race didn't exactly sound like her kind of thing, but getting to experience anything in Mamlakat Almas besides work sounded like heaven. The fact that it was at an ancient fortress? Just amazing. Some opportunities only came once, how likely was it she'd get back there again?

"What's in the bags?"

"I may have failed to mention to them that we'll be returning to the city daily to sleep here. I'm taking the other bedroom. And the other is medical supplies. The helicopter is waiting for us on the roof."

He reached out and tested the weight of the material of her linen trousers. "This should do for now. Thursday's location's been getting enormous amounts of rain this season. We might end up canceling if it doesn't dry up—just so you're aware." He called to Tahira, who came out, instructed her to take the other bag to the second bedroom, when to expect their return, then held out his hand to Nira.

"Rainstorms and flooding in desert country?" she asked, "I bet they're enjoying that."

"It's rare, but there are stories of rains like that, just not within living memory."

Within minutes they'd boarded the helicopter, donned headphones and were whisked heaven-ward.

Dakan said nothing, just let her gaze out the window at the sand below, at the roll of early morning light casting perfect curving shadows off the dunes.

He'd taken her hand a few times when they'd been in public, and Nira had always assumed it was a protective thing—that she was out with him so he felt responsible for her safety. Then things had changed, and he'd begun taking her hand in the apartment when they were quite alone, and she knew the gesture had changed. It was just for the pleasure of touching.

But once they'd been seated in the helicopter, he'd taken it again, and sat now with their fingers intertwined, resting in his lap.

His thumb stroked the outside of her thumb, something he'd only done in private before now. Even in the back of the limo no one really had been able to see what had been going on, but here in the helicopter there were people sitting oppo-site them, and they'd definitely see.

Something was different.

The crew could hear anything she said to him, with everyone wearing the headphones with their mics. All she could do was peel her gaze from the landscape and look at him.

His eyes were closed, his head leaning back against the headrest, but he wasn't asleep.

Something was really wrong.

The only way she could think to get his attention was to squeeze his hand.

His eyes opened and he looked at her, brows up, questioning.

Nira silently mouthed, "What's wrong?"

Dakan shook his head, gave her hand another squeeze, and laid his head back again.

No "Tell you later" or indication that his reluctance to talk was because of their audience. He just didn't want to talk about it.

"Tomorrow we'll be flying further this way, and on Wednesday in the other direction over the royal desert abode. It's our oasis."

"You own an oasis?" As soon as the words were out, she felt dumb. Technically speaking, they kind of owned the country. "Why do you keep a desert abode? Isn't the desert harsh and somewhere you wouldn't want to live if you didn't have to?"

He shook his head. "You'll see tomorrow. The desert is harsh, but it's also beautiful."

"Can I see the royal abode? Is it another palace?"

"Tents. Massive luxurious tents. It actually looks more like a camp village—there are servants who live there year round, they have their own tents."

"On the way back on Wednesday can we stop and see it?"

"There won't be time. That flight is long."

The villages they were traveling to held no promise of the architecture she loved, but they held the promise of glimpsing life for a normal person of Mamlakat Almas—something that would be closer to what he life could've been than what she experienced with Dakan. But the idea of a big luxurious tent? Man, she still wanted to see that. And an oasis in the desert? There were probably big palm trees and everything.

"Oh, well, it can't be that thrilling. Just green stuff amid the sand, right? No architecture."

"No domes," he confirmed with a tired smile, his head still back, his eyes still shut. His thumb resumed that rhythmic stroking, back and forth. It wasn't about pleasure. He was comforting her. Or maybe he was comforting himself.

Something was definitely wrong.

* * *

Little more than an hour later they landed a mile or so from a moderate-sized village she'd seen from above. A small clean car waited for them, and once the bags had been transferred, she and Dakan piled into the back seat.

Once again, within the confines of a vehicle, Dakan took her hand.

Two men sat in the front, and as one started driving toward the village, the other chattered away in such a fast, excited cadence that Nira only managed to catch a stray word here and there, but as they drove into the town, down the narrow streets bordered by squat clay-brick buildings, her excitement turned into something else. She realized how hard she'd begun to squeeze Dakan's hand only when he covered their clasped hands and rubbed.

The car rolled into what she could only assume was the market, which was a smaller version of the one Dakan had dragged her from on that first day they'd met.

"He says we're going to the big building on the left, and that we'll probably have a bit of a wait to meet with the healer."

"What language is he speaking?"

"It's Arabic, just a local dialect. You'll develop an ear for it by the end of the day. Listen for words you understand, and use them as guideposts to work out what the sounds would be normally."

Right. She couldn't even come up with words usually, figuring out what words these words sounded like? Pretty much the same skill.

Outside a squat, dusty-looking building the car stopped and their guide saw them inside.

"You wanted to see what would be familiar to people," he said, and she could feel the jerk smirking behind her as he spoke.

"Yes, I do want to see..."

The chattering man opened the door for them into a room choked with people. It couldn't have been more than four meters on any side, and there were only half as many chairs as were needed. People stood to wait, sat on the floor, sat together in one chair...

What could she do with this? She wanted to provide seating for anyone who had to wait at the hospital, not leave them to stand or sit on the floor.

Maybe low bench-style padded seats and creative use of the decor to build in places someone could perch...aside from chairs and couches.

Their talkative guide clapped his hands, getting everyone's attention, and then announced Dakan. "That's not necessary," Dakan said, just a little too late. Immediately people began rising from the floor and their chairs, an offer of seats coming from all around the room.

"We're going to have to sit," Dakan murmured behind her, "They're offering hospitality. It'd be rude not to accept."

Nira nodded and though it felt wrong she followed Dakan to a single wide, armless chair and then squeezed onto it with him. She made her thanks, then met the kind gaze of an elderly woman to her left and smiled while Dakan began speaking to people to the right, telling them all the good things he'd heard about this healer. Probably lying to charm them—she knew he didn't really want to include the healers with the doctors, but he made a good show of it. It was a common political skill.

But Nira had become so attuned to Dakan and his ways in the time they had known each other that she saw the stiff formality in the way he addressed these people. Even though they might not notice that his usual charm wasn't up to snuff, she could even feel where their bodies touched that the usually relaxed Dakan had gone rigid.

He claimed to like people, but the prospect of speaking to all these people made him feel uncomfortable.

When there was a break in Dakan's conversation, the woman to her left spoke and it took Nira a moment to work out what she'd said. He was right, once she found her guideposts it became almost clear.

Was she a princess?

"No. I'm an architect," she said, speaking as slowly as she always did, with lots of pauses to try and recall words. But those nerves she normally felt when trying to speak the language weren't there. Their dialect was different, so if she made a mistake or pronounced something in a way that sounded silly or childlike, they probably wouldn't notice.

"The Prince hired me to design a new big healing facility for the capital. He brought me here so I could see a good one."

The woman smiled and nodded, and it presented Nira with the perfect opportunity. She fetched her sketchbook and a pencil and asked, "Would you mind giving me your advice?"

When the woman nodded and gestured for Nira to continue, she asked, "If you were designing a new room to wait in, what would you do differently?"

Informal polling method, to be sure, but effective. Once the woman answered, another woman a short distance away added to what was said. Before long, she was getting suggestions faster than her pencil could keep up with them.

They waited a good hour before Dakan got to go back with the healer, though it didn't seem like it with all the conversation happening around him.

Once Nira had asked for opinions and started taking notes—taking the people seriously—everyone wanted to give their ideas. He spent part of the time translating for her as they spoke too fast for her to understand much.

It started out being about the waiting room, then went from there to other aspects of the treatment. People weren't as averse to the idea of Western medicine as his father and that barely used hospital made it seem. Infections were a big worry to them.

Before he even got back to speak with the man he'd come to see, he had made a note to text Zahir that he was right about the blending, at least for now. If nothing else, it'd help the people migrate to the new system to have the healers they were used to there as well. He just wasn't convinced that their father wouldn't wrestle control back to the healers no matter how it started out.

Once Dakan fixed a problem, he liked it to stay fixed. That rarely happened in medicine, but with physical ailments there was always something tangible that could be done. There were defined steps to take—do this, if it doesn't work or the situation's too advanced for this, do that. Escalating plans of attack to defeat a physical foe—an ailment, disease, or injury, and people usually didn't fight treatment.

Emotions were harder to fix, the emotional landscape like constantly shifting sand.

He should probably stop thinking of the hospital as something that would fix their problems. He couldn't guess what people—like Father—might do with it once they got it set up.

When the healer summoned him back, Dakan whispered in Nira's ear, "Will you be all right by yourself?"

She nodded and smiled over her shoulder at

him, a peculiarly happy expression for someone talking about work. And chairs.

"If you need me, shout my name and I'll come." He kept his voice low, took his bag and rose, leaving Nira to fend for herself with the people in the waiting room.

Over the next half an hour he discussed ideas to incorporate doctors into the current system without overriding the healers and about building a new country-owned facility to take the place of the current building, allowing more room for treatment and patients and those who came with them.

By the time he returned to the waiting room he actually felt pretty positive about the whole thing.

He spotted Nira right where he'd left her, and she gestured him over as soon as their eyes met. With his much lighter bag on his shoulder, he approached and crouched down to listen as she began to gesture to a mother with her sick child beside her. The little girl, no more than five, lay limply against her mother's shoulder, her face flushed and her eyes showing the splotchy redness of recent tears.

An ear infection, Nira told him. Something they hadn't been able to shake.

Normally, he would've passed by, not inviting himself to minister to someone else's patient, but he couldn't turn down a direct plea for help. Especially when he had the antibiotics that would help.

Over the next quarter-hour he examined the child, administered a loading dose of antibiotics, spoke to the healer about irrigating the ear, and went over the importance of taking all the antibiotics just as he detailed.

It was routine, so routine that he could've done it in his sleep, but it still made him feel good. Useful. Helpful. And something else...an emotion he couldn't quite put his finger on and didn't want to examine.

By the time they left the building he was actually looking forward to the next facility visit, even if it would be more of the same.

"That was something to see," Nira said, cutting into his thoughts. "You're good with kids."

Their guide had gone to fetch the car, which left him a moment to let his guard down with her.

"I told you emergency medicine was Zahir's territory, and that mine was the land of the simple family doctor." He could say that to her, but it wasn't an accurate test. "Keep in mind, though, that was my *second* patient. It's probably easy to be good with kids when you only see one patient every few weeks."

"Your territory?" Nira said. "That's the second time you've used that word with reference to what you or Zahir do. You say it like that, it sounds like these old dogs our neighbor had when I was little. I can't even hear that word any more without hearing it in Mr. Benjamin's voice: 'Don't mind Chester—he's just marking his territory.' You talk about your territory and I immediately get the mental image of you and Zahir running all over, peeing on everything."

He laughed so loudly, so suddenly that he scared people walking out of the healer's building. It was probably against royal protocol, laughing and treating patients in public. He pulled his gaze to the sky, then the horizon, looking for neutral ground, but the smile stayed on his face.

"Sorry. Sometimes I say things and everybody regrets it."

"I don't regret it. I'm just glad you said it in English." He laughed again, and their car pulled up so he opened the door for her. "Get in."

They climbed in and once they'd settled she turned to look at him again then reached up to adjust the hang of his *keffiyeh*, pushing back the white material that had fallen forward to conceal his face from her. "Did your talk with him go well?"

"It did, actually. And that sort of public meeting you held with the waiting room gave me a few more ideas. I'm going to run them by Zahir, but I think we've worked out some programs that will make things much better."

"Did he want to work with you?"

Dakan nodded. "Zahir was right, so long as it doesn't get corrupted and out of balance. Having both will be better."

CHAPTER NINE

THE MOMENT THEY stepped through the penthouse door that evening, Dakan pulled off the robe and *keffiyeh*. If he got to be here with her for a couple of days, he'd do it as freely as he could, squeak every ounce of pleasure out of their time together, no room for the negatives that crept in when he was alone.

Once he told Nira about Prince Jibril, the peace he felt with her would come to an end. That idea ate at him, made him want to keep her close for as long as he could. Made him spend all day ignoring the ticking clock because he didn't like how it made him feel.

He hadn't been thinking about a long thing between them anyway. But he wasn't ready for it to end yet.

"Do you need Tahira to clean your robes for tomorrow?" Nira asked, eyeing his exceedingly rumpled casual outfit he'd been wearing beneath. "Looks more comfortable than your usual suit."

Hearing her name, the housekeeper appeared, informed them that dinner was nearly ready, and spirited away the discarded clothing to launder.

Dakan flopped onto the couch and leaned back, closing his eyes.

Tomorrow. He'd tell her tomorrow. Tonight he'd enjoy the bubble of peace in this place.

"You look like you've just run a marathon," she said from very close by a short time later. "Or maybe like you're very drunk."

"Sleepy," he murmured, then opened his eyes to baggy green shorts and a T-shirt.

It wasn't revealing at all, but after spending so much time with her, and only seeing only her hands and face, the display of shapely tanned legs and the braless wonderland that was her chest... "You're the one dressed for bed."

"Yep," she said, sitting beside him, crawling under his arm and settling her cheek against his chest. "I need to ask you a question."

It was all very innocent, but it still made his mind race. She tucked her feet up under her and got comfortable.

"Ask away."

"You've been different today. I noticed it right away, and I thought at first maybe it was because you were sleepy, but it stayed with you all day. You're different when you're with people than you are with me. Actually, you're different with your patients too. Not just little kids, I don't think. I noticed it with the man at the hospital, but I didn't really put it together until I got to know you better."

He let his hand cup her shoulder, holding her there against him as they relaxed. "Different how?" He knew he behaved differently at different times, but he'd thought of the difference as upholding expectations—something everyone did.

"Stiff."

"With who?"

"Just with people you're interacting with. You even kind of do it here, not with me but with Tahira. You just suddenly stop being Dakan and become Prince Dakan. And then when you were with the little girl today you were Dr. Dakan, I guess. But he's more like regular Dakan than Prince Dakan. And when you were holding her and talking to her mother? It was really split. Your face changed, your voice changed—you were Prince Dakan from the neck up. The rest of your body was Regular Dakan, just a man comforting a child in distress. Like you carried and rocked sick children all the time."

"Prince Dakan is stiff? So I had a stiff head and a relaxed body?"

"Yes. You had a stiff head and voice and a relaxed body—what I could tell with the robes on. You hold your shoulders differently. I haven't seen that split personality thing happen before, but it definitely happened today." She tilted her head to look at him, then reached up and combed her fingers through his hair, which felt too nice to stop her from doing it, even if this cozy couch cuddle shouldn't be happening. "I thought you liked helping people have better lives."

"I do," he said quickly, and then paused to remember what he had been thinking at the time, but it was too much to think about when her fingers slid through his hair, soothing away the tension he'd carried today. "It was different today."

"Different how?"

"I feel obligated to be a certain way when I'm here, and I'm used to being another way when I treat patients—which I've only ever done in England. Here I've only ever been what was expected, or I tried to be within limits. I guess I don't know how to be both at once."

"Maybe you're just over-thinking it. Who says you have to be a certain way?"

"Everyone since I was small."

"I think, as a man, people will forgive you being a rascal more than they would a princess. You can rely on your cheeky charm with the masses, not just with people you speak with privately, or in other countries. You don't think they'd like the real Dakan?"

"I'm sure they would, but liking and respecting or following someone, feeling confident in their ability to lead your country? That's two different things. And I have to be ready to be...what I desperately don't want to be."

"Which is what?"

"Heir, should something happen to Zahir. People need to have confidence in me, just in case. When they don't, that leads to succession instability. The Al Rahal line is very old. We survived different empires as a sometimes puppet kingdom until the Ottomans began to branch into the area and our king made a stand to avoid being swallowed up again. Which is what the race is about tomorrow." He caught her wrist to pull her hand back to his chest. "You remember the story about the Lego house and the trebuchet?"

"How could I forget?"

"The part of that I didn't tell you was that it

was my idea. Sort of. My actual idea was to use these old battle axes and chop it up. Zahir upped the game and went for the trebuchet."

"And got into trouble for it."

"We would've gotten into trouble for the axes too, but it wouldn't have been nearly as amazing as the trebuchet."

"So he made getting in trouble worth it?"

"He just did it better. I'm not saying that because I'm looking for sympathy. I know my limitations, and I think it works out well this way. There are things he's better at, and things I'm better at. So we have a wide range of stuff covered."

"Territory?" Nira mouthed the word up at him.

He squeezed her, groaning, "Would the word 'claim' make you happier?"

"Yes. It sounds like an old-fashioned gold prospector in a gold rush somewhere. I like it."

"Noted."

"But you're saying that being a prince is something that Zahir is better at?"

"Yes. Being a leader. Taking a tiny idea and making it powerful, and having the ability to inspire people to follow him through it."

"But you don't like being a follower, and you don't want to be the leader."

He grimaced. "When you put it together like that, it sounds very egocentric and spoiled. Selfish. But maybe it's true. He's the leader, I'm the follower, and he should never let me lead him astray."

"And you wanting him to come back is noble, not just about freeing you to go back to England."

"See? You did it again. Made it sound bad. Maybe I shouldn't talk about this stuff. Better to not upset the status quo." Only he wasn't the one who'd upset the status quo. It was this showdown between Zahir and Father—which Zahir had apparently won, and yet *he* was still here.

She slipped her hand free of his and slid it up his chest, the good tingle left in the trail of her touch commanding him to open his eyes and look at her.

The sweetest eyes met his. Beautiful, yes, but they had the kind of warmth that made being seen by her feel tangible, made him want to stretch out and have her look at him whole.

"I'm asking you questions to make you think, not to criticize you. Because I want to stay here for as long as I can, and I want you to stay too. I also want you to be happy, but something is making you unhappy."

She did. He could see it in her eyes. The prospect of telling her about her father was making him unhappy right now, other than that he'd had a pretty good day. His position didn't really bother him, he was just trying to answer her questions. Answering them let him pretend he didn't have other important things to say that she'd spent her whole life desperate to hear—the dread that ate at him when he considered her future should Jibril acknowledge her and accept her as an Al-Haaken was hard to ignore.

Her hand slid from his chest to his cheek, and she leaned up to press her lips to his brow. The soft, lingering kiss started there then wandered over his cheek and eventually settled on his mouth. Gentle, languid, it was as unhurried as it was thorough, kissing with no ulterior motives. His body reacted. He couldn't feel the slide of her tongue against his without wanting to take her to bed, but the slow, easy pace drained tension from his body, giving him comfort he'd needed all day.

By the time she lifted her head he didn't know whether to stretch out and cuddle her or take her to bed.

The second being the less likely option for now, he pushed her hair back, tucked it behind her ear and looked into her eyes again.

Peace won. He wrapped his arms around her, and once she'd settled against his chest they waited for dinner in easy silence.

The race to the Immortal Fortress was a morning affair, but even getting up to fly at first light couldn't put a damper on Nira's excitement.

Tents littered the desert all around the ruin, camps of families who'd come to enjoy the races, along with stables for the camels.

The helicopter touched down and an SUV waited to drive them the short distance to the ancient citadel. Today Nira couldn't touch Dakan— he was there on behalf of the King, and propriety wouldn't allow those little displays of affection, though she could sit with him to watch the race.

The fortress had one hole blasted in the wall facing the border, but the rest of it was remarkably intact. Stones that had fallen from the hole had long ago been moved to the side, though never carted away, the damage never repaired. The corridor and staircase up to the roof held firm. It was damaged, but it kept standing strong and true.

On the roof, a platform had been erected with two large ornate chairs—thrones, really—and a smaller, simpler chair facing them, all set beneath an awning to shield the royals from the sun.

Dakan took the larger chair, gestured for her to sit, and refreshments were immediately brought.

"Why are we on the roof?" she asked in a whisper when people had moved back enough that she didn't feel so conspicuous speaking to him.

"Because the King of Mamlakat Almas was on the roof, having his breakfast on that day. He'd sent his army to another part of the border to engage the Ottomans and hold them out. We'd have been happy as allies, but when did being conquered by anyone ever sit well with a small country, even one with shared faiths? The day before the battle, a messenger arrived at first light on camelback, scaled the wall, delivered word to the King, whom he'd seen on the battlements."

Nira sat, utterly absorbed by Dakan's story. She could see it all in her mind, and somehow felt so much more attached to it than she ever had to history classes at school.

"What did the King do?"

"Gave him food, water, a change of camel, and a message to summon his army to White Stone Castle." He pointed down to the building they sat upon. "The Ottoman army arrived ahead of his, but the King, his Queen, and all the people in the castle armed the cannons and fought with whatever they had. Hot oil they'd used for cooking."

"The Ottomans were the ones who blew a hole in the wall?"

"And the cries of the Almasian army behind them turned the battle around. There were terrible losses on both sides, but Suleiman the Great continued his march to the gulf, sidestepping Mamlakat Almas, and we've remained independent since. The third chair will be for the first racer to reach us and climb the rope."

"There's a rope?" She'd missed that part. "What do they win?"

"A fat purse of gold coins, and the opportunity to serve a year as the King's Messenger at functions in the city and small ceremonies—of which there are many—where they bring a message and read it out to whomever is in attendance."

"When did they start calling it the Immortal Fortress?"

"Not for another century, I don't think. They expected it to crumble in where the hole had been punched, but it never has. The desert tries to swallow it up now and then, they sweep out the sand a couple times per year, but it's still in great condition. The story now is that as long as it stands, the country will never be invaded from the north. The Kings began carrying out the race in the eighteenth century as a remembrance that the actions of one person can help the whole country."

As soon as he said the words, the smile he'd worn changed...like he'd only heard his own words after they were out of his mouth.

Nira reached over to touch his hand, even though she knew she shouldn't, and he squeezed her hand then let go abruptly and turned to the organizers. "Are we ready to begin the race?"

"All has been made ready, Highness. The racers are on standby."

Dakan nodded and gave word for the cannon to be fired.

By Thursday morning, Nira had recovered from their trip to the Immortal Fortress, and was over her excitement at traveling to far-flung villages.

Wednesday's trip had been long and exhausting, though when they'd flown over the oasis she had regretted that she hadn't been able to go there. Maybe she could convince him to take her once the hospital building began.

As a tour and a chance to see the country, it did

not fail to amaze her, but she didn't learn anything else on that visit that would help with the design.

Prince Dakan had kept busy, talking to people and trying to be whatever was expected of him, and she could clearly see the differences now that she was looking for them. Prince Dakan gave test vials to a man and ordered samples of the water taken from the therapeutic springs for testing. Regular Dakan would've gone into the springs himself to test them, or something else active. Prince Dakan didn't reek of vigor and activity like he did when no one but her was looking. He'd be easy to resist if she hadn't come to actually care about him enough to look beyond his royal persona.

He was still a puzzle, though.

He wanted to make the lives of his people better, and he didn't want anyone looking to him for leadership or decision-making, but he also didn't trust the decisions made by others.

The trebuchet incident kept coming up, and always with a different emotion attached to it. She wasn't sure whether it was a happy memory or a sad one any more.

All she knew for sure was that he was a man in conflict with himself, but she didn't know whether he ever expressed those conflicting opinions to his family. She'd never met the King, but intuition said he'd be domineering—that was perhaps what a king had to be. The idea of Dakan having any kind of discussion with his father, where he was actually listened to, seemed far-fetched. But Zahir had struck her as someone easy to talk to, and Dakan obviously loved his brother. He could talk to Zahir. They might not agree, but just talking things through resolved most problems.

Like with her mum. Nira wanted to talk about the situation with her father, she just didn't feel like she could. She didn't want to cause pain, but also she didn't want to deal with the frustration that came any time she tried. If they could just talk things through, if she could just understand...

"Nira?" Dakan said at her side, getting her attention.

She looked across the back seat to the open car door where he stood, bag in hand.

"We're here."

Facility number three. At least the geography was different here. Tuesday and Wednesday had been dry and sandy with little in the way of visible rocks. Today they'd made it to the area that had been experiencing lots of rain, but arrived right after the rain decided to move out and the ground had drained most of the water away.

The facility sat at the base of a rather steep cliff, which didn't seem safe. She grabbed her bag as she climbed out, and paused to look up. "Do they suffer from falling rocks?"

"The ground here is very stable. There hasn't been so much as a tremor in Mamlakat Almas for decades." He gestured for her to walk ahead of him. "Rain is even a rare event here. Except this season. But there's no rain today, and no signs of flooding. I think we're safe."

She stepped inside and moved in far enough to survey the room and let Dakan enter with his huge medical bag. There were fewer people in the waiting room than had been at the other two, and a number of chairs sat empty, perhaps due to the rains.

One empty seat was beside a very pregnant woman with a baby playing at her feet. He twisted to look as they came in, and started crawling toward them. Before the woman could catch him, his speed increased along with the volume of happy gurgling baby noises as he made a beeline right for them.

The alarmed woman scooted forward in her seat

as she tried to find her center of balance so she could stand.

"Wait, I'll get him," Nira called to the woman, bending to scoop up the baby before he got trampled on in the close confines of the waiting area.

As soon as she had him in her arms, the baby immediately reached for her scarf and began tugging at it as Nira walked back to the distraught woman. "I believe this is yours." She tried to disentangle his fingers from the scarf, which now was horribly skewed on her head, and smiled despite the mess she knew she must look.

The woman reached for him, but it took both of them working together to get his little grabby hands unwound from the silk so Nira could put him down.

She chanced a look at Dakan, found him smirking and offering her no assistance, at least until the healer saw him and took him straight back.

"He is quite strong!" Nira said, when they finally got him back into his mother's arms.

"Forgive us, Princess. I think you must look like my sister to him," she explained.

Nira reached up to try and right the mess, but found it just wouldn't seat again. "There is nothing to forgive. And I'm no princess. The Prince hired me to design a hospital for the capital. We're touring places of healing so I can design the hospital well."

She made her way through what she wanted to say more easily than she had been doing, finding the words she wanted—or something very close to them—without long, tense silences. What she couldn't find was a way to tie the scarf appropriately again without the aid of a mirror.

Time to give up. She unpinned the colorful silk from where it covered her neck and unwound it. The best she could do on her own without a mirror was to drape it over her head and tie it under her hair so that her head was covered.

Smiling to smooth over any awkwardness, she began the same conversation she'd held at the first two facilities. This time she led with, "I was going to ask you what you'd change to improve the waiting room, but I think I have an idea. Somewhere for little ones to play safely?"

She reached for her bag to get out her sketchbook and pencil to take notes, and felt a rumble in her seat. The hair on the nape of her neck stood on end, brushing firmly against the knotted silk when she turned her head to look around for the sound.

Earthquake? Dakan said...

The sound of earth moving crashed outside, and she dropped her sketchbook. Everyone looked as alarmed as she felt, so this was definitely not a normal sound.

They should get away from the cliff, outside the building.

By the time the thought solidified, most of the other people had risen and rushed toward the door.

Yell if you need me, Dakan had said, as he always did.

Nira screamed his name, then pitched to her feet. Her legs felt encased in half-set concrete, but she was up.

Without a word, she took the baby from the woman's arms and anchored him to her chest. People piled out of the only exit; no one stopped to help them. She hooked her free arm under the woman's closest arm and strained to help her to her feet.

Something smashed into the outside of the side wall, then several more somethings followed in rapid succession, each issuing a resounding crack.

The baby screamed, and Nira did too as the surface of the wall bowed inward, cracks appearing from the center.

Behind her, she heard Dakan shout her name.

As she looked back, the wall crashed in and the floor fell from beneath them.

Dakan felt the building shake, heard the rumble, and then screams came through the wall separating them from the waiting room.

The elderly healer, dumbstruck, gripped the frame of the window beside him and stared at the door.

Power surged through Dakan on a wave of fear, and he sprang from his chair. A moment later he had the door open to the waiting room. All he could see was dust in the air, and light behind it where there shouldn't be light.

"Nira!" he yelled, in time to see the other side of the building collapse and three silhouettes disappear.

It was her. He didn't have to see her clearly, he felt it in the roar ripping through his belly.

His lungs seized before he could call out again.

Dust. Cover your mouth.

Ripping the robes over his head, Dakan paused long enough to shred the shoulder seam of one arm, pulling it entirely free of the garment, and then tugging it over his head until it covered his face from his cheeks down.

Once out the door of the consultation room, the floor seemed intact to the front exit but looked dodgy. He tested it with one foot, but it bowed beneath the lightest pressure.

Their way was blocked.

Get the old man out; find Nira.

Grabbing his bag, Dakan used the hard bottom to push the glass out of the frame in the solitary window, then tossed the bag through.

"Come on, we have to get out," he said, offering a hand to the elder healer. It took both hands to ease the frail man through the window. A minute later he had the bag in one hand and the man's arm in the other, and was pulling him away from the broken building.

Outside, people had gathered, most of whom he recognized from his time in the waiting room.

His heart in his throat, he searched every grimy face for Nira's on the chance that she'd crawled out. Nothing.

All of his people were worth worrying about, and he was concerned for them too, but for Nira... Terror clawed at his guts.

The pregnant woman wasn't there either, or the baby.

Leaving the bag with the old man, Dakan rushed

back to the front of the building to survey the damage. Big rocks. He'd told her they were safe.

They hadn't come through the roof, though.

To the left of the building he saw it, a slide of earth at the bottom of the cliff face behind another house that had been damaged, and a path leading from that mound of wet earth to the rocks piled against the side of the healing center.

A moment later he had his satellite phone out and was calling for the helicopter.

The call made, he began organizing people to take a head count, find out who else was still inside. And once that was done he doused his severed sleeve mask with water from his bag and put it back on, creating a slightly better filter.

He was going in.

Nira awoke to the sound of a baby crying in a high frantic keen that brought everything rushing back.

He lay face down across her belly. She could feel him there, angry, squirming and scared. His cries sounded wrong to her somehow, raspy and wet. Something else lay over one of her feet. Something soft and warm.

She opened her eyes, dust and dirt falling in and causing them to stream as she tried to see what was going on. Picking the baby up, she moved him so he lay down her chest with his head by hers in the vain hope that being face to face with her might comfort him.

That done, she curled forward, trying to look toward her feet, but another coughing fit took her, shaking her and the baby until she got past whatever threatened her airway.

He cried louder. She wanted to cry too, but she still had an inventory to take.

One more effort and she lifted herself enough to look towards her feet. One of the woman's legs lay across hers, not moving.

Was she breathing? The view to the woman's torso was blocked by debris, and she couldn't hear the sound of breathing above the baby's labored, choking cries.

Dakan. Where was he? Was he down here too?

What was she supposed to do? Should she stay put and not collapse the rubble more, or just take a chance on getting herself out, regardless of what happened to the rest of the building if she went plowing through?

She laid her head back down, one arm still wrapped around the baby. She squeezed him enough to let him know she was there, then set to rubbing his back, trying to shush him as she took inventory on the room and tried to wake the woman.

She hadn't asked her name. What kind of person met someone and spoke with them but didn't ask their name?

"Hello?"

"Hi?"

"My friend?"

She tried several more greetings, trying to get some answer from the woman.

Nothing came. No movement.

Not far above her, maybe five feet, floor joists jutted from the part of the building still above ground. It wasn't deep enough to be a basement. Crawlspace of some kind? Some of the joists remained connected to the floor and angled down to touch the bare earth beneath. One lay across her other arm. She wriggled it free without too much trouble but it soon began to throb.

More dust and dirt showered down on them, and the baby's coughing cries began to sound like gasps for air.

"Nira?"

Dakan's voice, loud and rough with fear, carried through the opening above to her, even above the sound of the baby's cries. She patted his back, trying to get him to calm as she called back to Dakan.

"I'm okay, I think. But the baby can't breathe!"

"I hear him. Is your scarf still on?" he yelled back.

She squirmed to pull her other arm free from the tight space it was wedged into. When she did so, one of the joists directly above her, one that had one end planted to the right of her hip and the other still wedged against the remains of the flooring, fell a few inches.

"The floor is coming down!" she screamed, kicking her legs free from beneath the woman's and shooting her feet into the air to catch the bottom of the joist.

"Dakan!"

He didn't answer. God, where had he gone? He hadn't even finished his instructions about the baby.

He'd asked about her scarf. She pulled it off with her now free hand and shook it out as best she could, then put it around the baby's face, holding it with one hand as the other patted his back to try and help him clear his lungs. She didn't know what else to do.

Her mother had been right. She'd come to the Middle East, and now she was going to die here. Like stupid tourists who got stupid ideas about seeing exotic foreign lands and wound up being crushed by spontaneous building demolition.

The baby coughed hard once more and began to breathe more easily.

"Nira?"

He'd come back. He'd come back.

"He's a little better, I think," she called back. "But his mother hasn't moved. Or answered. And the floor! Dakan, the floor is going to fall if I let go…"

He called from above again, "I'm going to climb down to you. I found a way from the healer's consultation room."

The consultation room?

That was…

She looked through the dust-clogged shafts of light and got her bearings. She'd fallen straight down, so the consultation room Dakan where had gone was…on the other side the floor she was holding up.

"No! Dakan! No! Don't come that way!"

"There's no other way," he called back.

"Don't come that way. I can't hold more weight.

Most of it's being transferred to the ground, but if the angle shifts, it's going to come down!"

She waited a few seconds, preparing to tense her legs for all she had. Was he going to do it anyway? Was he still up there?

The baby started screaming again in earnest now that he'd had a chance to catch his breath, and pushed at the scarf she kept pulled over his face.

"What should I do? Can you see another way?"

Nira lifted her head to look past the rubble and the dust.

"How much of the floor is intact in the waiting area?"

"It's not safe to walk on. I tested it."

"Get to the crawlspace. Find an access door. Or knock a hole in the foundation below the consult room and come in below the floor."

She patted the baby again and made a shushing sound.

"Hurry!"

CHAPTER TEN

OUTSIDE THE HALF-COLLAPSED building men approached, running with tools in hand. When Dakan relayed Nira's suggestion to the men, they went round to the far end of the building to begin knocking a hole in the foundation.

Dakan left them to it and went to pack a small bag to take down with him. Face masks. Water. Small respirator. Bandages. His pathetic penlight, which seemed completely unequal to the task of lighting up a low, dusty basement. Crawlspace. Whatever she'd called it.

He made it back to the building in time for them to start pulling rocks out of the opening.

One large stone came, then some smaller ones. He couldn't even hear over the noise whether or not the floor was still up, whether Nira was calling for him, whether the baby was even still crying. Metal on stone, metal on stone…strike after strike until an opening big enough for him to squeeze through appeared.

"No one else come in until I say so," he instructed. It'd benefit no one to have more hurt if there was some way around it. Scout first. Make evacuation decisions after.

Dakan pulled a mask on and crawled through the hole and down to the packed earth floor about a meter below.

He immediately heard the crying baby.

When he'd slithered his legs through, he got back up and reached out for his bag.

He pulled the mask off his mouth so she could hear him. "Nira?"

"Please, hurry!" she called back immediately. He put the mask on and turned on his flashlight, then stood as much as he was able to move at a crouch to where the floor had fallen in.

The crawlspace wasn't a solid open rectangle— there was a corner in the earth, leading to what he imagined would appear L-shaped if viewed from above. Along the walls leading to the turn, there were shelves with jars, cans and dry goods… which meant there had to be stairs somewhere. He found them when he rounded the corner, still intact despite the floor above partially covering them, built into the side of what must have been a trapdoor concealed in the waiting room.

Just to the left, he saw the woman's head, then bent to crawl under wooden boards to reach her.

"I found her," he called to Nira, checking for a pulse and then listening to her labored breathing. "She's alive. Can you see her?"

"Her legs were on mine."

He dropped the awkward bag so he could crawl over the prone woman, where he found Nira on her back, her feet braced against a thick, precarious-looking board above her, and a screaming baby on her chest.

The air suddenly felt even denser than the dust, heavy and hard to breathe through. Every instinct told him to drag her and the baby out of the way and get them out of there. But the woman... There had to be a way to get them all.

"If I hold the floor, can you crawl out with him?"

"I don't think so. My arm hurts. Take him. Take him out and come back."

She was putting on a brave face, but he could hear fear making her voice wobble.

He couldn't look at her arm yet, not until he got back. He also couldn't leave her here without any help. If nothing else, he could help her breathe better. He whisked his mask off, secured it over her mouth and tucked behind her ears.

"I think I saw a faster way to get the woman out. I'm going to get them to knock another hole in the foundations at the corner of the room right next to where the floor fell. Is that okay?"

She paused to think. Maybe it wasn't just his mind that had become sluggish... After a few long seconds of looking in the direction he'd mentioned, she nodded.

"Should be." Her words were muffled, but he could understand her. "Crawl over me with him, it'll be easier to get through that way than climbing over her. Don't put any weight on anything wooden."

"I'll be right back. Hold on a little longer," he said, swinging one leg over her and then the other, then picked the baby up from her chest, clamped him snugly to his chest with one arm, stuck the flashlight in his mouth, and crawled through with the still screaming baby, retrieving his bag along the way.

It felt like it took him a year to make it to where he could stand and walk at a crouch back to the opening.

Once there, he passed the screaming baby through, following it up with the bag, and directed the men to make another hole in the foundations at the back of the building, and gave the best location he could, along with another order to do it carefully because rocks tumbling in could hurt someone. The stairs would make it easier to carry the woman out without so much danger of dropping her.

When he finally made it back to Nira, her legs were shaking and she looked pale. He grabbed her wrist and checked her pulse. It was fast and her arm shook just as her legs did. "How do I brace the wood?" he asked, just as the sound of the pickaxes starting to attack the foundations came to them. It sounded like the right area at least.

Pushing the mask back, she got a deeper breath and said, "Big rock. Plant it at the base where it touches earth."

"How big?"

"Like a bowling ball with angles instead of smooth."

"Okay." He'd seen them pulling stones like that out of the foundations. This sent him hurrying back to the opening once more.

He heard rocks falling in at the other site, but there wasn't anything he could do about it now. He gave instructions to the men still at the hole, and they produced three rocks that were almost the right size, but not quite.

Dakan took the two biggest and hurried back.

"There aren't any that big. These two were the biggest..."

She looked at them, considering. "Wedge the small one under the space between the wood and the dirt, then put the big one behind it. When you have it, tell me and we'll test it."

Dakan had to backtrack around her head to reach the end. He did as instructed, roughly shoving the rocks into the earth in the hope they'd slide slower.

"Take your feet away."

He tilted his head to get a visual of her and watched as she relaxed her legs but didn't remove them. The board started to slide again and her legs kicked back into position, taking the weight once more. Strain showed on her features and in her groans.

He pushed on the rocks. "It's not working."

"Step on it. Use your feet. Legs are stronger than arms."

That wobble of fear turned into a full voice tremor that shifted the sounds into some kind of

wrongness that alarmed him further. He had to
get her out of there.

Dakan braced himself against the intact rock
foundation, one foot on the big rock he'd placed,
and ground down with all his might.

The board actually slid in the other direction,
enough to lift the tilted floor a few inches.

"Did you lift it?"

"Yes," he said, then, "Is that bad?"

"No. I'm letting go…"

Once again she relaxed her legs, but this time
the boards didn't immediately start to fall.

"It's holding. Can you get up?"

He rounded the treacherous board, careful not
to touch it, and reached for her unhurt arm to pull
her through the hole to where the woman lay. Nira
nodded toward the woman. "We should get her
away from the—"

At that moment daylight spilled in through the
foundations where the men were making their
holes.

"I don't even have a neck brace for her," he muttered, shaking his head.

"Is the baby okay?"

"I don't know." He didn't know if either baby
was okay, the one he'd carried out or the one still

in the woman's womb. But they had a way out close by now. He climbed the stairs and helped shove the rocks outward. When the hole was big enough, he stepped down the few stairs, grabbed Nira and hustled her up to the hole. "You first."

"You need help with her. She's heavy."

"Your arm is hurt. Don't argue. The other men will come and help me move her."

He grabbed her hips and thrust her up and through the hole, and someone helped pull her through, then two men came down to help him with the pregnant woman. She still hadn't regained consciousness. He took out his stethoscope and listened to both mother and fetal heartbeats for a minute, counting. "Hers is a little slow, but the baby's holding on."

Within a quarter hour the helicopter lifted off with all his patients on board. Nira held fast to the baby even though her arm hurt. With some effort, she kept him from removing the makeshift hearing protection Dakan had fashioned with cotton, gauze pads, and tape. There was nothing else Dakan could do for anyone right now, but he'd get them to the trauma center in Dubai at least.

With one hand keeping the unconscious woman's pulse monitored, he watched Nira and the intensity with which she watched the baby in her arms. She'd swaddled him snugly enough to mostly immobilize his arms, and watched his chest move since the headphones muffled her ability to hear his breathing.

So much for his plan to tell her everything tonight. His family would just have to understand. Nira wasn't moving to the palace yet. Once the woman and baby were off to Dubai, he'd call his mother to let her know, then examine Nira's injuries.

No one could expect him to lay all that on her after the day they'd had.

Tomorrow would have to sort itself out.

The helicopter touched down at the airport and Nira had to turn the baby over to the crew so they could transport him and his pregnant mother to the hospital in Dubai. It'd taken Dakan promising to send the helicopter back to the village to fetch the father for her to let go of him.

The one bright spot from it all was that the injured woman had briefly roused during the flight to the capital, and now they'd both receive the kind of medical care in another country that they should've been able to get in their own.

When they were gone, Dakan put an arm around Nira and steered her toward a car that she hadn't even seen arrive. As soon as she'd climbed in, sleep overtook her and the next thing she knew, he was gently rousing her outside the dreadful hospital.

"What are they going to do here? I don't want to be treated here."

"I'm going to X-ray your arm." He swung the door open and clamped an arm around her waist to get her out with him.

She moved with him. It was too hard to put up any real resistance right now. "You said there wasn't an X-ray."

"I had a temporary set up until the hospital is finished, and imported a couple of technicians."

"I don't think it's broken."

"Good. Let's double check."

She didn't want to double check. She wanted to go back to the flat, run a hot bath, and soak away the pain and the grime she carried in equal measure. But she got out, because getting out and getting it done would get her to that hot bath faster. "Where did you put it?"

"Behind the building in a bus, like the mobile diagnostic clinics they take to the villages in the

UK. We'll move it inside when the room for it is built."

Inside the lobby, her gaze naturally drifted in the direction of the current remodel. Long pieces of plastic sheeting had been secured to the ceiling and hung to the floor, discouraging people from going into the surgical theater and keeping the construction dust somewhat under control.

So it was really happening. Not that she could see much. Dakan led her the other way and soon she was in a curtained bay, being handed a gown.

"I don't need a gown for an X-ray."

Dakan continued to hold it out to her. "A building fell on you, Nira. You had a beam fall on your arm, and you used your legs to keep the ceiling from collapsing. Put the gown on so I can examine you. Unless you want the other doctor on duty to do it."

"I don't want another doctor to do it."

"Good, because I wouldn't allow it anyway."

"Can I get the X-ray done first?"

"I'm looking for other areas to screen."

Nira sighed and turned around, "Unzip me, then. But I'm only stripping down to my underthings, then you'll look at me and I'll get dressed again before we go to the bus for an

X-ray. I'm not walking around in a hospital gown with my bum on display."

"Fair enough," Dakan said. So obviously he could compromise a little.

She felt the zip slide down until his knuckle brushed the small of her back. It was the simplest touch, but a wash of awareness that hit her. He might as well have licked her.

It was the wrong time and place for that kind of reaction. They were destined to be together, for at least a time...and she wanted it. She just didn't want it in a hospital bay.

To hurry things along, she tugged on the shoulders of her dress to dislodge the garment and wrestle her arms out of it.

"Is it ill fitting?" she heard him ask from behind her. "You're jerking at that material like it's stuck to you with glue." His hands closed over hers and he took over, easing the material down much too slowly. She wanted this over with.

Princess seaming in the simple green dress allowed it to fall to the floor as soon as the zipper passed her waist and opened to the hips. She stepped out of it, picked it up, and faced Dakan.

No power on earth could make her look at him, though. She knew he wasn't looking at her like that right now, but the day had wiped out her confidence. Confidence required a steadier, calmer mind than she had right now. And probably a bath first.

She fixed her gaze on the ceiling and waited as he angled her toward the light. Even then she couldn't make her heart slow down, and with the feel of his hands on her body—even moving clinically as they were—it took all her concentration to try and breathe normally.

Carefully he ran his hands over her from her collarbone down, skipping the breasts, but cupping his hands again around her ribs to continue feeling down her. He hit sore spots several times, and she was grateful for them. At least the soreness helped negate the tingling warmth that radiated from wherever his hands touched her.

A few questions, blessed yes or no answers, and he turned her around. "You have a lot of bruises but your sore arm is the worst of it. I'm not sure it's not fractured."

Now that he was behind her, it was safe to pull her gaze from the ceiling. She looked down her body and suddenly felt much worse. No wonder she was sore. "Please tell me some of that's dirt."

"Some of that's dirt," he obligingly repeated,

whether he meant it or not. Then his hands were in her hair, brushing the back of her neck as he dragged the heavy mass over her shoulder. His fingers traced down her spine and that feeling raced back through her body, with goose-bumps following closely behind.

That reaction was hard to miss, and he missed nothing. His hands slowed and his touch changed— instead of feeling with his palms and the tactile working side of his fingers, she felt the light bump of knuckles and then a soft, gentle smoothing of what could only be the backs of his fingers down the last portion of her spine.

"I need..." His voice sounded strangled and he took a breath, cleared his throat, and tried again. "I need you to lie down so I can examine your belly for signs of internal bleeding."

Was that some sign of desire? Or had he just inhaled too much dust in the rubble? "My belly doesn't hurt," she murmured weakly, not trusting her voice to remain steady.

"Please, Nira, I need to make sure you're all right."

Something in his voice made her look over her shoulder at him. He looked worried and more than a little upset, probably the only thing that could make her agree.

A moment later he'd helped her to the exam table and was palpating her abdomen. The air between them had changed again, now somewhat awkward because of the sensuality clogging the air and his attempt to remain professional despite it.

Once satisfied, he picked up her dress and then helped her sit up, slipped it back over her head and helped her get into it fully.

"X-ray of arm," he said, and once again led her out of the curtained bay. "Then we'll go back to the penthouse and rest."

The penthouse had never looked so good to Nira. Tahira eyed them both worriedly, but spirited away the battered sketchbook they'd dug from the rubble.

Nira gave a slapdash attempt to wash her face, at least getting what was around her mouth clean, but she'd gotten into something sticky along the way and so when she returned and sat down to dinner it was with a still grimy face. Eating was likewise mechanical. She didn't taste a bite, but once she'd had enough and tried to rise, she really felt the soreness setting in.

A mildly frowning Dakan watched her as she rose, like she might fall at any second and he'd need to catch her.

She touched his shoulder as she passed but didn't say anything. If she wasted a drop of energy on words, she'd probably pass out and drown in the bath.

A few minutes later, when the water was adjusted as hot as she could stand it and she was ready to get out of the dress, she remembered the zip. Negotiating it with an injured—but thankfully not broken—arm was inconceivable.

She opened the door to call for Dakan, and nearly ran into him. "I was coming to ask you for help."

He gestured her back into the bathroom and once there moved her hair off her back again and unzipped the dress.

This time he didn't let her do any of the work to take it off, just edged the sleeves back down her arms, and let the dress fall.

"Thank you," she said, her state of near nudity along with her conflicting emotions giving her enough nervous energy to speak. "I didn't say that earlier, did I?" She turned toward him and murmured, "If I had clothes on, I'd hug you. You didn't have to come in there after me. After us. You probably saved my life. Thank you."

She let herself look him in the eye, so he'd know she meant it. He'd risked himself and was still looking after her, and it wasn't just doctorly instincts. He cared.

That knowledge eased the worry from her mind and she stepped in to lean against him, taking whatever comfort and strength he offered.

When he'd appeared beside her in the rubble, all she'd been able to see had been his eyes above the material covering the lower half of his face—dark pools of worry and tension, and that look hadn't left him until after he'd examined her and been satisfied she wasn't badly injured.

Her relief had come while she'd still been under that beam, the moment she'd looked into his eyes. He hadn't left her down there. He'd risked himself to crawl into the dark insides of a collapsed building for her.

What she felt for him was real. It was love, and she knew it now as surely as she'd known he'd get them out of there. Her feelings were real, and so were his. It might not be love that he felt for her,

but he'd put himself in jeopardy to protect her—
and a man like that could never be a betrayer.

This wasn't the same as her mother's Middle
Eastern folly. They might never have anything
more than these few weeks together, but she'd
take whatever she could and let it sustain her af-
terward, not tear her down. Nira was a builder,
and all building required a leap of faith.

Dakan held her for a moment, then eased her
around in his arms until her back touched his
chest again, and he wrapped his arms back around
her while burrowing his nose under her hair.

The same hands that had medically pressed and
explored her belly not an hour ago now flattened
out, fingers splayed, pressing her back against
him.

"You don't have to thank me," he finally answered, his words caressing her ear, then nuzzled
and kissed the back of her neck.

Immediately, goose-bumps returned, and she
tilted her head slightly forward, giving him whatever access he wanted.

His hand slid up her belly, found the front hook
of her bra and flicked it open, then let his hands
slide up to cup and gently knead both breasts.

Needing to get rid of the rest of her clothes, she

pulled her arms free of the bra straps. He released her and knelt to slide down to her knickers, finishing undressing her as he couldn't before.

When they touched the floor he turned her toward him again, at eye level with her sex. He pressed a quick kiss atop the small mound of flesh, rose and helped her into the hot steaming water.

This was happening. He needed her too, she could see it in the pained look in his eyes.

It only took him a moment to shed his ruined clothes, baring a body that was beyond perfection to her eyes. Tall and muscled, brown skin, fine black hair over his chest, and down over his belly, a slowly engorging manhood that left her feeling short of breath...

Dakan grabbed towels from a nearby closet and washcloths, and put them all within easy reach before stepping into the bath with her. "Lean forward, *habibi*."

He settled in behind her, and she turned toward him, tucking her nose under his chin as she snuggled in.

Gently, he stroked her hair away from her face and rested his chin on her head. Her dirty head...

This was definitely happening.

Nira would've never thought that having a man bathe her could be sexy, but the tenderness in his eyes confirmed all she believed to be true. It was love, though that sexy intensity he could flatten her with appeared when he helped rearrange her on his lap so that she straddled his thighs, and she saw a flash of something playful when he had to work to get off a particularly stubborn patch of sticky grime on her cheek.

When he'd rinsed her face clean, he took another cloth, scrubbed it over his face, wiped it clean, and then urged her back so she lay in the bath between his legs, him bent over to run his fingers through her hair.

Heavy sensuality blanketed every touch. He washed and rinsed her hair with care that left her feeling cherished. Sooner than she'd have liked, he'd washed them both clean and drained the tub.

"I don't want to get out yet."

"Neither do I." He turned the water back on as soon as the murky dregs drained away, adjusted the temperature, and set it to filling again with them in it. "I just want to be able to see through the water."

Before the water even reached her hips, he'd moved her higher on his lap, high enough that he could complete promises. His mouth dragged across her still damp skin, sucking, licking, nipping, but over any bruise he merely stopped to stroke his lips against the battered flesh.

Reverence and love, heat and need. It left her feeling breathless and aching, and it gave her strength to come together when her energy had long since left her.

CHAPTER ELEVEN

DAKAN HADN'T INTENDED on taking Nira to bed, or to bath.

Well, he had, but as soon as he'd learned who she was he'd tried to talk himself out of it and had stayed away as much as he could. It hadn't helped.

Dakan never deprived himself of whatever woman he wanted—he didn't know how.

It'd be too simple to blame some primitive need for conquest, like touching and tasting her was fun. But that's not how it was. The usual excitement paled before the hunger to consume her that ripped through him even while he wanted to walk away.

He leaned her back, turned the water off, and then pulled her more fully against him, letting his hands slide over her slickened skin to find and squeeze sweetly plump curves as he finally got her mouth to his.

Water sloshed in the tub as she leaned away, arching perfect breasts toward him, her green eyes dark and pleading, her fingers curled into the hair on the back of his head, urging him forward, her voice low and throaty. "Do you want me to beg?"

Dakan shook his head. "You don't have to ask for anything." He kissed his way to a taut nipple, then sucked it greedily into his mouth.

A tremor rattled her and she ground her sex against his hardness so that he felt her heat, her wetness...slicker than the water.

Releasing her nipple, he pulled her back up against him and then flailed with one hand at the side of the tub. Where were his trousers?

"What are you looking for?"

"Condom," he panted, and she leaned out to find and pick up his discarded clothing. A moment later he had the foil package in hand but no dexterity. Wet fingers didn't want to open it up.

"Is it safe?" Nira asked breathlessly. "In the tub, I mean?'

Dakan thought for a moment, then, locking one arm around her, he dragged them both out of the bath. Her legs wrapped around his hips and gripped him, and he rolled her to the rug. Nira grabbed a towel, wiped her hands, and took the condom from him. A moment later, after employing her teeth to get the job done, she had it out and strong little hands unrolled it onto him.

It wasn't fun. It wasn't a game. The pleasure of her hand squeezing and stroking him was too much, too heavy, too raw. He pulled her hips back to his, and nudged his way into her. Not a virgin, thank merciful God. He didn't want to be the first. He wanted her to have memories of other men, in case this seared into her the way he felt it searing him. He didn't want her to love him.

"Is this all right?"

His voice sounded strangled even to his own ears. She nodded, grabbed his head and pulled his mouth back to hers, her soft body taking everything he gave her, returned every kiss, every thrust.

Not the first. And he prayed not the best even if he couldn't imagine anything better.

Don't love me. The words ran round and round in his head, in his heart, a silent prayer he let echo and repeat even as he wanted it ignored.

Don't love me.

Don't love me.

Don't love me.

He felt her tighten around him and then the blessed clenching that shredded the last of his self-control. He breathed in her every gasp and the words she whispered into his mouth. Words he'd ignore. Words he'd pretend not to have heard.

When the tide had passed, with what little strength remained in him Dakan rose with her still sealed to him and staggered to the bedroom. The bed bowed as he laid them both down and started all over again.

She couldn't mean it. It was just the emotion of the day.

She didn't really love him.

Rapid, near-frantic knocking on the bedroom door pulled Dakan out of sleep. Nira, still groggy from all the sleeping they hadn't had, grumbled something and tucked her face back in against his chest.

That level of urgency at a bedroom door was always worrying.

Dakan reluctantly pulled himself from the bed, grabbed a discarded blanket from the floor and covered himself before opening the door. Tahira stood there, looking so wild-eyed he knew immediately what was wrong.

He hadn't taken Nira to the palace last night,

and though the message he left had said as much, someone had come to collect them.

"Make tea," he said, just to give the frazzled-looking housekeeper a direction, then ducked into the second bedroom—never so thankful for a hall-way in his life. Pajamas laid out for him the night before still lay on the bed. He grabbed the bot-toms, tugged them on, and went to face the mes-senger after making certain Nira's bedroom door was closed.

So Mother had come to collect Nira. Could've been worse.

He rounded the corner and found his father standing at the wall of windows, overlooking the city.

"Father," he said, mentally scrambling to work out what to say. Something he could never do was speak candidly with the King, and it was probably that difference Nira saw in him from when he was a royal envoy to the times he could be himself. He could talk to his mother, be honest, but he al-ways felt the weight of expectations in his father's presence. "I left a message. She was banged up pretty badly when the building collapsed on her."

The King turned and leveled a steely look at

him. "And you needed to stay with her all night to monitor her health?"

He knew. So much for not speaking candidly. At least it'd be easier to know what to say if he didn't run his thoughts through that father-filter first.

"I just needed to stay with her. It was a bad day."

"You made her feel better, then?" the King asked, shaking his head. "I have come to bring her to the palace. Where is the maid?" His voice rose and Dakan felt that familiar headache blaze into existence—the one he always got when his father got demanding.

"I'll bring her later." He tried again.

Tahira came scurrying and bowed, and the King went on as if Dakan had said nothing. "Get the girl up. Get her dressed and presentable. Then pack her bags. She's coming with me."

"Father, please." Dakan held a hand out to Tahira. "She can't handle you swooping in on her today." He lowered his voice to a loud whisper. "I haven't even told her yet. Let me tell her first."

"Tell me what?" Nira's voice came from the hallway and he turned to see her peek around the corner, looking worried and exhausted.

Dakan immediately moved to guide her back down the hallway.

"Prince Dakan Al Rahal." His father's words stilled his feet as effectively as they caused his head to throb. "You will not be alone with her."

"I'm sorry," he whispered, taking her hand to bring her back into the sitting area, but in the next heartbeat all will to do as expected evaporated.

Anger rose and he faced his father. The man had never even met Nira before today. *He* was the one who knew what was best for her. "I will be alone with her. She doesn't need a royal audience for this—it's too much. I'm taking her to her bedroom to speak privately."

"I'm putting an end to this impropriety."

"Yes, you've made that perfectly clear," Dakan bit out. "All celebrate! We've reached the end of impropriety! But I'm still going in there with her. Unless you want to execute your wicked son today, stay here. What can you possibly think is going to happen if we're alone together? We just need to talk." Dakan didn't wait for an answer, just returned to Nira to guide her back to the bedroom, intent on ignoring his father if he shouted any argument.

Surprisingly, none came.

He closed the door, focusing on her extremely worried face.

"Am I being kicked out of the country because we spent the night together?"

"Of course not."

"He probably thinks I've got no morals now that we've..."

"Don't worry about him." Dakan urged her to sit on the edge of the bed and sat beside her, taking one of her hands in his. Speaking candidly with Nira had been easy from almost the beginning, but words that would hurt her didn't come easily. "Between the times we kissed, I realized I couldn't pursue you. Last night should've never happened because I know who you are."

"I'm no different from who I was when we met," she said, a frown line creasing her forehead. "What does that have to do with the King? And why does he want you to bring me somewhere?"

"He wants to take you to the palace and not as punishment. You didn't do anything wrong. It's about who you are. I know who your father is." He spilled the words in a rush.

All traces of anger left her face, and she went from tense and pained to every feature frozen with shock. He waited an eternity for some sign that what he'd said had sunk in.

When he saw hope bloom in her eyes, it made it everything harder.

"You think you know who he is, or you actually know him?"

He'd been unable to help himself last night, and he couldn't today—if she cried, he'd do whatever he could to stop her.

"He looked familiar when I first saw the photo, but I couldn't place him. The more we talked, the more convinced I became that I knew him, but I still couldn't remember from where."

"Why didn't you tell me?"

"I didn't want to get your hopes up. What if I couldn't ever remember? There was also the small matter of our project. I selfishly didn't want to distract you. We were making good progress."

"Who is he? Is he a bad person? Is that why you look so worried?"

"He's one of the younger brothers of the royal family of Tabda Aljann." Even saying the country's name made him want to grit his teeth. The rivalry was fairly petty, he had no real grudge against them other than disliking the knowledge that their king, Ahmad, had once wanted his mother—more than thirty years go. If he could've picked another family for Nira, he would have.

"He's a prince?"

Dakan reached for her other hand—she looked like she needed the support. "Yes." The closer he got to telling her everything he knew, the more he needed to touch her. As soon as the words were said—as soon as they themselves left the penthouse—she'd be completely untouchable to him.

"Seems like you can't swing a stick without hitting a prince around here. I want to meet him. What's his name?"

"His name is Jibril." That was at least easy to answer. The rest... "I don't know if you should meet him. You might not even want to. There's some things you should know first."

Some of the hope dimmed, and she turned her hands over so that she could curl her fingers around his in return, and nodded for him to continue.

"He's married, for one."

"Of course he is. It's been a long time. I wouldn't expect him to stay single all this time just because Mum did."

"No, *habibi*. He's long married."

"It's been a long time since they were together."

"His eldest son is the same age as Zahir."

He watched her slowly start putting it together. "Has he been married more than once?"

"No."

"So he was married when he was with my mother."

He nodded.

"He *cheated* on his *wife* with *my mother*?"

Dakan nodded again.

"Then he sent her away."

"I don't know the whole story, but that's my suspicion. I haven't spoken to him. I'm not even certain how someone could diplomatically broach the subject with him."

"Maybe they found out she was pregnant, and he sent her away to protect her. To protect us," Nira said, though the look in her eye confirmed her words as a last desperate attempt to try and salvage something of the situation.

"Maybe." He said the word she wanted to hear, but from what he knew of Prince Jibril, Dakan doubted his intention had been so noble. And he knew for damned sure that his father's intentions were at least slightly skewed by her lineage. If she were an unacknowledged daughter from any other country, he wouldn't force her to move to the palace.

Nira fell silent as she worked through everything, but the look in her eyes made her seem lost, and in that moment all he wanted was to shove his father out the door—and do whatever else might give her the peace the past twenty-four hours had stolen.

But he couldn't do that.

"There's more…"

"I don't know if I want to hear more right now."

"I don't want to say it either," he admitted, releasing her hand to wrap his arm around her, and grudgingly added, "but I'm under royal order to do so."

She didn't say anything else, but both hands went to her face to scrub over her cheeks and eyes.

Get it all out. This piecing out business made it longer, and longer was worse.

"I figured out who he was when I was speaking to my mother. She was telling me about her trip, countries they'd visited, and when she mentioned Tabda Aljann, his name just sort of appeared in my mind. I remembered where we'd met and talking to him. My mother noticed me falter, that's why you can't stay here now."

"I still don't understand why the King wants me at the palace. I don't want to live there, I'll be a basket case twenty-four seven. You've seen how it hits me... Besides, my equipment is here. We can't go wheeling that monstrous plotter into the palace, it'd probably scuff something up."

"I don't want you there either, though I'm sure you can get used to being in the presence of your architectural family." He jostled her shoulders, then remembered she was still hurt when she winced. "Forgive me. I don't know how I forgot to be gentle with you today."

"It's okay. But I'm staying here. I need to work now before I lose track of the new ideas. Like a place for physical therapy in the future, which would be the perfect place for the therapeutic baths if that water composition can be manufactured. I'm ready to get back to work now."

"You don't have a choice, and you need to rest for a few days anyway."

She stood up suddenly and was back out the door, leaving Dakan to scramble after her.

"Nira..."

"Why do you want me there?" Nira asked as soon as his father came into view. "You don't even know me."

"You're a royal daughter of House Al-Haaken, even if you are unacknowledged. I won't have you living alone here in the capital. It's impossible."

Nira wasn't as hesitant to speak candidly to his father as Dakan was.

"I'm not going." She stepped back further, and it was then that he saw tears in her eyes.

"You're in Mamlakat Almas, I have ordered your relocation." His father's voice rose then and Dakan stepped between them, as if that could block the loudness of what would follow. "You cannot remain in a country and disobey her king. If you leave now, your contract will be voided and you'll never be allowed back within the borders of Mamlakat Almas."

"Father, I can handle this." Dakan shook his head, staring hard at his father. Dakan understood what this meant to Nira, and what it probably meant for her future.

She reached up and pushed her hair back from her face as if it were some spider web she'd just walked through, then stepped fully behind him. He felt her forehead impact the center of his bare back and her hands grip his sides.

"You should've told her earlier in the week, not

put it off so you could bring her home and forni-
cate with her."

"I know! And that's not why I brought her
home—that just happened. I was being selfish
again, because that's what I do, right? Zahir's the
generous one, and I'm his shadow. But the time
I spend with Nira here is the only time I enjoy
spending in the country. I knew as soon as I said
these words all that would change."

He saw the spark of interest flare in his father's
eyes and before he could say anything else, Dakan
gave his head a sharp shake.

When the look stopped him saying anything
marriage-related, Dakan turned to Nira and pulled
her to him. "You'll be allowed to come during the
day and work here. You're not going to be a pris-
oner, *habibi*. You're going to be an Al Rahal ward.
So you'll have that tour of the palace finally, and
you can look at as many domes as you want to for
as long as you want to."

There was more, but he didn't think she could
take any more right now.

He didn't have the heart to say it now anyway.
He just hugged her and let himself smell her hair
one last time, and then nodded to Tahira to take
her to dress.

Without another word to his father, Dakan packed up Nira's laptop, sketchbook and pencils, and then went to change his clothes.

CHAPTER TWELVE

NIRA COULDN'T DECIDE whether to feel some kind of pride at the revelation of her birth, or terrified that people were now making decisions about where she could live and what she could do.

But in keeping with her desire not to get exiled from the country for disobeying the King, she rode along in the back of his car with the two Al Rahal men in a silence so heavy it could've made bricks and built the Hagia Sophia!

How different it felt from her first journey to Qasr Almas. She couldn't help but look at Dakan, and she knew he felt her gaze. The muscle at the corner of his ridiculously square jaw bunched harder when she looked at him for any length of time.

Just when she thought she might scream just to break the silence, they pulled onto the winding road that led to Qasr Almas, and she watched the Diamond Palace come into view.

This could be a massive mistake. The King

had threatened to cancel her contract if she ran screaming for the airport now, but maybe that was the price of her freedom. She could find another job once she got home, probably. Though who knew the range of an angry king? She'd been hoping for positive references once this job was done, not for her client to send something scathing to her employer to follow her around until the only architecture job she could get would be designing garden sheds.

If she was honest, despite what Dakan had told her about her father, these people were the only ones willing to give her information. Maybe Mum would... *Oh, hell.* She'd have to tell her mum where she was living, if nothing else.

The car rolled to a stop, men opened the doors and the King exited on the side of the entrance. She and Dakan left via the opposite door, and he finally looked at her again as he extended a hand to help her from the car.

How many times had their hands linked in the past weeks? Even before last night, touching his hand had felt like an intimacy she'd never shared with someone else. Even before she'd known she loved him. But now he squeezed her hand, and the sorrow she saw in his eyes almost broke her down.

Carefully, he guided her hand to the crook of his elbow so material separated their skin and escorted her through the door.

A beautiful woman in flowing robes and glittering jewels came out of the palace, her arms open. The Queen she instantly recognized—Dakan had her eyes. She spoke Arabic to Nira straight away, and pulled her into a painful hug.

The Queen either didn't know about them, or she was very good at putting on a friendly face.

Either way, Nira wasn't going to bring it up. She returned the hug, then fumbled her way through the social gestures she'd have made with the royals of her own country—curtseying, inclining her head, pretending all was well and that nothing ugly lurked between the three.

"I shall show you to your suite personally. The healer is waiting for us there. Dakan said you had a building fall on you yesterday! I must say you look decidedly better than I feared you would. But you are stiff and sore, the healer will help." She gestured for Nira's bags to be brought. "I expect you and I will spend the next week in the healing baths."

"All day?" Nira asked. She hadn't subscribed to Dakan's idea that she needed time off—she was just playing along. "I need to work on the hospital." She glanced back, but Dakan was nowhere to be seen.

"Yes, Dakan said you are doing wonderful work. They're already building the suite for our Adele's coming birth, so you can have some time to recover. He said you saved a baby boy, landed with him on you to cushion him from the fall? Then held up a roof by yourself?"

Nira climbed the stairs as bidden, doing her level best not to look at anything but the next step. Getting distracted by the walls would be bad, or the carved balustrade running along her peripheral vision. She did break down and take hold of the rail about halfway up, slowing her pace somewhat and lengthening the likelihood that she might get overly emotional about the carvings and pillars dancing up the walls.

"I didn't so much plan the fall as that's how it happened. And it wasn't a roof, it was part of the floor. I really did very little. Dakan saved us. He got everyone out."

At the top of the stairs they turned down a short corridor, and she was shown into a suite that for the moment made her forget her pain and worry. There was no way to keep from looking. The bed was a platform built into the wall with a thick pillow-like mattress on top. There was a window with an arched top and deeply carved seat jutting from beneath where one could sit and gaze out at the sea...

What were they talking about? Work. She was talking about work. "I don't want to take time off." Right. Pay attention to the room later. Don't look right now.

She made herself focus on the Queen. "The tour gave me so many ideas, I don't want to forget anything."

Say something nice about the palace. "But if there was anywhere I needed to lie about and not do work, this would be the room for me. I don't suppose there exists any documentation about when the palace was constructed? Their methods or, well, anything that happened during its building?"

"There are scrolls. Your Arabic is very good, you should be able to read them."

As the bags had been dropped off, the healer motioned for the door to be closed and then he and a maid who introduced herself as Samina began to remove her clothing. Despite quiet protests, she was stripped down to her bra and knickers, and the healer began a careful inspection of her bruises.

"Dakan said nothing's broken. He made films of my arm. No internal injuries."

The man nodded. "But you are not well. Your muscle has been damaged, and you have need of soothing. It is right that you shouldn't work for a week, and you must take the healing baths daily. Wear no restrictive clothing. Will she be in robes, my Queen?" He directed the last question to Leila.

"Yes, there are many, and Adele's should fit her well enough. Their coloring is different, but they will serve until new ones arrive."

"New robes?" Nira asked, trying to keep up with the rapid Arabic. Hers was improving all the time, but she still could get very lost when overwhelmed. "May I sit?"

She had no idea what was expected of her, but standing there in bra and panties didn't help her keep focused on the words flying around.

The healer gave another order for the restrictive clothing to be removed, and gave instructions on tonics the *attar* would send and how to properly take them.

"Let Samina dress you and then you shall rest today. This afternoon, after the sun weakens, we shall go to the healing baths. Oh, Nira, I'm so glad you've come to stay with us. Dakan says you will want tutoring, and spoke of how much you loved the trip to the Immortal Fortress. I'm sure you'll find scrolls and books in our library to satisfy your every question. Perhaps we can visit a mosque when you're rested, or some of the other ancient buildings in the city."

Had Dakan already handed her off to his mother in that regard as well? Technically it would fulfill his promise to make sure she got the chance to explore when the project allowed, but before it had always sounded like something he'd participate in.

Samina led her to bed and she dutifully climbed in. She was tired. Maybe she could take some time to pursue her own goals finally. If Dakan came to yell at her to get back to work, at least she'd see him.

"Thank you, Your Highness. I'll try not to be too much trouble."

"You may call me Leila, Nira, though I'd still call Fatiq by his title. You are our guest and I'll not have you pinned down by a title when we shall talk so often." The woman went to look out the windows, and then gestured to the maid again, gave instructions for the windows to be opened and for Nira to be left to sleep until dinner. Then she turned back to Nira. "I'll leave you to your rest. Welcome to Qasr Almas."

Everyone filtered out of her suite and Nira got out of the bed to find her phone. She fumbled through her handbag, flicked it on and immediately texted Dakan.

Does your mother know? And can she not be told if not?

I don't know if she knows. Try to forget it.

Forget that they'd been caught, or forget what had happened?

She sat down on the bed again and tried to rewind what Dakan had said to her earlier.

"Last night should never have happened."

And "I can't be with you."

So it was over?

She lifted the phone again and texted.

Will you be at dinner?

No.

Breakfast?

I'm not going to be in the palace much. Rest. Work next week.

Or next month. I have access to a whole library here.

She waited for ten minutes for him to rise to her bait, but realized with a sinking feeling that he wasn't going to. Why did all her relationship arguments come down to texting?

Not trusting herself to stay calm if she rang Dakan, she walked back to the doorway and turned so she could get the whole room in an image. In an adjoining bathroom she took a photo of herself in robes that obviously didn't belong to her.

She sent both pictures to her mother with captions: *My bedroom. My new outfit...*

Then she dialed her mum's number. If that didn't make her pick up, nothing would.

She'd had enough of treading lightly.

The following Monday, having convinced the healer that she was fit enough to sit quietly at a desk and draw pictures, Nira let herself back into the penthouse. Tahira came in from the other room, and bowed upon seeing her.

"I'll be coming daily to work on the hospital," she said, moving directly to the desk so she could unload her laptop and sketchbook, all she'd had to work with since being moved to Qasr Almas.

Tahira offered tea in response, accepting without questions. At least that would be the same.

Speaking Arabic had started to feel normal. She no longer had to think in English then mentally translate to make herself understood. She could thank Dakan for that, if she ever saw him.

Not that she could count on that in the near future. Dakan was off doing medical system stuff. He no longer came strolling in whenever he liked, no matter how much she wished he would.

In the days since she'd been relocated, she'd occasionally seen him from a distance when the helicopter had picked him up or dropped him off. Texting him had worked that first day, but had garnered nothing but silence since then.

For the first time in her life Nira sympathized with her mother's romantic trauma. If this was how she'd felt...

She could ask her mum. Since she'd sent the photos, her calls were always answered. Her mother had even given a modest amount of information about Jibril. Apparently, knowing the man's name had been the key.

He was her father. Check.

He'd sent Mum home when he'd found out she was pregnant. Check.

They'd met in Tabda Aljann when she'd accepted a position as an air hostess on the royal family's new fleet of jets. She'd fallen for him on a long flight she'd worked to Australia. All that was new information.

Thanks to her studies, she knew Tabda Aljann meant *Paradise Begins* in one of the local dialects. It didn't sound like a bad place to go but she'd learned her lesson. Just because something felt good, it didn't mean it was good for her.

Mum had probably felt much worse.

Or maybe she'd felt better. She'd come away with Jibril's child, at least.

How would it feel to have Dakan's child?

Tears rushed to her eyes before she could banish the thought.

What a stupid thing to ask herself.

She may understand her mother better now, but she wouldn't become her. A broken heart could be mended, or it could be left to putrefy.

Nira was a builder.

Inside, she might still feel like she was flat on her back in that crawlspace, holding up floor joists with her feet, but she wouldn't stay that way. She'd get out from under it and rebuild, which was what she was doing now—getting on with life, designing a project that would advance her career, laying a foundation for future projects to be entrusted to her.

Foundations were never easy. To construct them properly you had to dig...and dig and dig and dig...until you had blisters and raw, bloody hands. When you got far enough down to know your building would be on steady ground, only then could you start building.

She just hoped her heart would hurry through feeling raw and blistered. A week had passed since she'd seen Dakan, and she still felt she could barely take things hour by hour, that some minutes were longer than days.

It had been just over a month since she'd come to Mamlakat Almas. Zahir and Adele had returned and the royal family had begun to ready itself for a celebration of their nuptials. Nira stayed in her room and made long, frequent visits to the penthouse. One future wing for the hospital had now been designed. She tried to deliver the plans to Dakan for approval, but he didn't answer her messages. After three visits to knock on the door of his suite in the hope that someone would drag him to the door, she'd finally given up and sent them via the servants. He signed them and send them back the next morning.

It was like she'd become completely invisible.

Leila, who Nira had figured out knew everything that had gone on with Dakan, still treated her with kindness, still welcomed her on the evenings Nira felt she could no longer avoid dining with them without appearing ungrateful and rude. The King was the one who didn't seem to know what to say to her. He'd ask the obligatory questions about the hospital, and once she'd answered he'd nod, make some sound of approval, and eat his dinner.

She made herself more scarce after their arrival.

The importance of the hospital made people excuse her workaholic approach to it. She actually wanted to meet Adele, but the idea of seeing someone in married bliss with one of the Al Rahal brothers...

Maybe she was becoming her mother after all.

They spoke daily now, and she couldn't tell if

it was because of her new address and the fear it triggered, or because Nira's fresh, new heartache bonded them. Not that she discussed it much. It was her last bit of emotional currency, which she'd definitely need to get to the very bottom of her Father Mystery.

The morning of the fourth day since their arrival, Nira was finishing tying her hair up in one of the many beautiful scarves Leila had provided, wanting to be out the palace door before everyone got up—as had become her practice—when a knock came on the door.

An inevitable thrill followed as with any knock—hope that it was Dakan. She wanted to run, her feet demanded speed, but she made herself walk. She knew better. Dakan didn't knock.

A pretty blonde woman stood there, smiling, on the other side.

Adele.

Cornered.

"Good morning. You must be Adele," Nira said, speaking English for the first time in weeks. For lack of any idea of how to greet the woman properly, she offered a handshake. "I'm sorry I haven't been around." The idea of having to explain made her eyes burn, and she gestured quickly to the room. "I've been working. Please, come in."

To have time for her emotions to calm, she walked across the room and opened the drapes then the windows.

"The mornings have nice breezes here," Adele said. "This was my room when I stayed as Leila's nurse."

Suddenly, Nira remembered Dakan saying that his mother had been ill, and it brought her a pang to think of their previous confidences, now a thing of the past. "I trust she's better now?"

"She is. Fully recovered." Adele perched on the window seat. "A selection of gowns is being brought to the palace today. Leila asked me to make sure you'd be here as you haven't anything to wear."

And just like that, her plans for the day changed. Breakfast with the Al Rahal women. Shopping. Maybe some studying later if she was lucky.

Adele had made it sound like a request, but it really wasn't one. It came from the Queen, and if the Queen wanted you to go shopping with her…

This was what Dakan complained about. Even if she still wanted to shake him for his utter abandonment of her, she'd begun to understand his feelings and they hadn't even asked all that much of her.

Dakan's itinerary for the day left him without anywhere to go to avoid the palace at noon when everyone would be milling about. He should've taken a car to his morning appointment. Then it might've taken the whole day.

The sound of women laughing caught his ear as he approached the garden, intent on getting to his wing before he was spotted. He recognized his mother's voice and who was probably Adele. Would Nira be with them?

A smart man would've kept walking, not stopped to try and see her. But, God help him, he wanted to see her.

He just didn't want her to see him.

Keeping close to tall bushy palms planted in artistic clumps and lines around the garden, Dakan stopped, ignoring instincts telling him to run.

The three women sat in an arc of three chairs and before them another woman held up a gown for their inspection.

His mother finally had a daughter to dress for parties. And also Nira—Mother probably already felt attached to her even without the bonds of matrimony to tie them.

Her dark hair hung over one shoulder, thick and braided with a ribbon woven through it to match her robe. Hair that soft should never be bound up.

Mother and Adele appeared to enjoy the dress viewing, but Nira sat with such a blank expression, despite the blistering noonday sun, he felt an unpleasant coldness seep into his limbs.

Of course she wasn't happy here—though he couldn't be sure whether it was due to her new constraints or because he'd disappeared from her life.

Right. Enough of this. He couldn't bring her more except further heartache by sticking around. If she saw him, it'd only reopen that wound.

He hurried to the exterior door of his wing and immediately went up the inside stairs and directly back out to the second-level battlements. He'd be able to see her from there. She'd never think to look up. He could look his fill, regain control, then get back to business tomorrow.

"Yes, Nira will try the green ones," his mother said, clapping her hands and gesturing to two different green gowns—one emerald and one pale green that reminded him of her eyes. She'd look magnificent in it. But then, she'd look magnificent in any of them.

Mechanically, Nira stood and held her arms out for the gowns. "I'll just go to my chamber."

"No...there is a screen behind us, use that."

Dakan looked down and that cold pit in his middle heated up. If he stayed there, he'd be able to see her changing.

A gentleman wouldn't spy on her like that.

A gentleman would walk away, or never have let it get this far to begin with.

She stood for a long moment after the gowns had been placed over her arms until his mother asked what was wrong. Nira finally asked for the lavender dress instead.

So her will was still there. He could take some comfort in that.

The gowns were swapped out and she trekked over to the screen, hung the dress on one section of it, and began stripping off her robe.

Look away. Now would be the time to look away.

He'd seen her before, of course, but...

The silk slid down her arms and past her hips to float to her feet in a puff.

The bruise on her arm had faded a lot. At least

he could calm his mind with that knowledge. She was healing. He hadn't broken her body even if he was certain that he'd broken her heart.

She unzipped the gown and stepped into it. A moment later she had it on—save that zipper down the back. The memory of her zipper, the brush of her soft skin against his knuckles...

He was just torturing himself.

Rounding the screen with the back held together, she turned her back for Adele to zip and looked up. Their eyes locked over the short distance. Anyone else might've looked away from him, but Nira held his gaze. In her eyes he saw everything also currently churning through his insides. Desire. Sadness. Regret. Resignation. But something else—the way she held herself, the lift of her chin... Feelings he didn't feel right now. Strength. Determination.

She might sit quietly and do what she was told, but the woman had a steel core.

Adele finished with her zipper and bade her turn to face the Queen, and only then did she look away from him, turning her back on him as well she should. That was what he deserved, and what would be best for both of them.

He turned away as well, and went to lock himself inside until tomorrow came and another trip would rescue him from the lead deadening his own center.

He had to stay away, though he wanted to do something for her. Not an apology so much as give her something he knew she wanted.

Women in Mamlakat Almas enjoyed using henna for special occasions. All except Mother, who could never hold still long enough for the henna to settle, so she would never think to supply a henna artist to Nira. But Nira had mentioned loving the art. He could send her a henna artist without claiming the gift. Provide one last experience in her quest to discover her cultural heritage…anonymously.

She need never know it was from him.

CHAPTER THIRTEEN

DAKAN HAD DREADED the celebration since everything had happened with Nira, but was there any part of his life in Mamlakat Almas that he didn't dread now?

The medical care overhaul. He liked working on that. Having something useful and important to do was the only thing that kept him sane. Last month he could've said Nira, but in the past couple of weeks he'd felt dread for her every day. He dreaded what her life was shaping up to be, whether she'd caught onto it yet or not. He dreaded not seeing her, even as he did his best to avoid her.

The formal ceremonial acknowledgement of Zahir and Adele's union and prayers for blessings concluded, Dakan tugged the sleeves on his tux straight and walked into the ballroom for the private party with the family's closest couple hundred friendly dignitaries in attendance.

The Al Rahals, as hosts, were supposed to dress the part, but Dakan had resolved to stick with what he felt comfortable in, and to the burning sands with anyone who disagreed. The rebellion he'd avoided in his youth had finally caught up with him. There wasn't a single agreeable ounce left in him. No more acting simply to meet others' expectations. It had never served him in the past anyway.

He meandered to the side to an out-of-the-way spot where he could loiter and observe entering guests—and wait for Nira's father. One of the Al-Haaken would be there to represent their family. Mother had claimed not to know which, but he'd seen the lie in her eyes.

It'd definitely be Jibril, and Dakan was going to have a good long talk with him. He'd do what felt right. It started with the tux, and in the fairy-tale land of his mind ended with him and Nira hopping on a jet to London away from everyone who could cause them grief. Maybe there he could sort out relationships—how to have one. Probably not, but the fantasy was nice.

Nira came through the archway leading to the garden. Even with her head turned away from him and her hair covered, he knew it was her. She'd selected that lavender gown. The long sleeves and high neck may have hidden her skin, but it showed her shape. He didn't need to see her face, the hurt and determination he'd seen there the last time had burned into his mind.

The twinge in his chest had him turning away.

He stepped around a massive potted plant where she'd be less likely to see him, and refocused on the archway.

He couldn't undo his actions in the last weeks, but maybe he could prevent her father from doing further damage. Impress upon him the importance of civility with Nira, and disabuse him of any notion to abscond with her. He'd be civil but blunt. Not raise his voice. It was as far as his civility could extend in the matter.

"Why are you hiding in the bushes?"

Zahir.

Dakan cast an eye over his brother—the good one—regally clad in the expected robes.

"Plotting my escape," he murmured. He remembered the coffee in his hand and took a sip.

"I don't know about escape, but you're plotting something, by the look of you," Zahir said, moving to the other side of him and leaning one shoulder against the wall, demanding his attention but not quite blocking his view of the door.

"It's Nira's first big event. I don't want to take the fun out of it for her."

Zahir nodded slowly. "She sent me the plans for the hospital, what have been approved so far."

"They're rather remarkable, aren't they?" Dakan still pored over his set, even after he'd signed off on them. "You did well, hiring her."

"And you did too in actually carrying it out. I looked at the other proposals you wrote, for the Air Ambulance teams, traveling physicians, and the arrangements you made with Dubai and Qatar to use their hospitals during the build. Excellent ideas. Have you worked out proposed budgets for start-up and to maintain the service?"

Jibril swept in, blanking out everything Zahir had just said.

He needed to move if he was going to get to the man before Nira spotted him. Dakan turned back to Zahir and asked, "Can we talk about it later? It's your celebration. You should still be with your wife. It's her first big event too." He patted his brother's arm, and stepped around him to divert Jibril before he got too far into the crowd.

He intercepted him at the beverage bar and offered a hand. "Prince Jibril, I was hoping you'd be attending. Spare to spare, could I speak with you a moment?"

The man smiled at the greeting, and took Dakan's hand, just as he'd expected. The two families had been doing this dance long enough to know the steps.

Dakan shook his hand, though he wanted to break it. It might be jumping to conclusions, but that didn't mean the conclusions were wrong.

"It would be my pleasure."

They moved to a quiet area by the wall, and Dakan snatched his phone from his pocket, eager to get this over with.

"Do you remember this woman?" The photo of Nira's parents came up on the screen.

The man's eyes narrowed, all traces of the fake friendliness there vanishing. He twisted Dakan's cellphone so that the photo faced the floor, where people would not see it.

And looked angry.

"I see that you do. Were you aware your union produced a child?"

"What concern is this of yours?"

Now evading the question.

"Have you become entangled with this woman?" Jibril recovered his façade, but anger remained in his voice, his words. "This photograph is quite old, she is what the Westerners call a cougar now?"

Dakan didn't have the patience for this, but he wouldn't rise to the bait. He'd calmly deliver his message—a technique he'd been taught he actually approved of. The art of diplomacy didn't usually involve threats, but he'd learned how to modulate his voice during twenty-seven years of lessons.

"No, Al-Haaken, the child is my concern. Did you know about the child? She's here tonight. If you'd like to avoid her, it'd probably be a good idea if you left. That'd also be my preference in the matter. If you stay, you will address her respectfully. She looks like your family, so you wouldn't be able to miss her. Be a gentleman and we won't have any problems." He smiled, showing his teeth in the most socially appropriate manner possible.

Jibril knocked Dakan's phone out of his hand with a quick swipe. It hit the floor hard, and he made sure it was broken by slamming his heel down on it, shattering the screen.

"This is not your business, boy."

Clearly Jibril didn't appreciate Dakan's attempt at diplomacy.

He got exactly two steps away before Dakan was after him. Another three steps and they were at the beverage bar. As he rounded it, Dakan grabbed Jibril's wrist hard enough to spin him, but they'd kept things quiet enough so far that not many people in the room noticed their mild confrontation.

Jibril turned and Dakan stepped in, his hand still locked about the man's wrist. "You will only speak to her with cordial civility. Are. We. Clear, Prince Jibril?"

He could've just nodded, and that would've satisfied Dakan. There were a number of things he could've said without the situation escalating.

But Jibril's face turned red, his volume rocketing up so he all but shouted, "Unless you're the whore's son and not the good Queen's, leave it."

The sharply spoken words finally roused the interest of people in the ballroom, but all Dakan could really see was what might happen if they took Nira to Tabda Aljann. Was this kind of attitude the reason Mother had turned their king down? Did all the Al-Haaken men treat women that way?

If Jibril knew about the relationship between Nira and himself, would he call her a whore?

That was the thought that pushed him over the edge.

All the rage and helplessness that had been simmering in him since that morning she'd been denied him roared to life, and Dakan's fist flew.

No amount of warning him to be good to Nira would work. This was not a man who would even respect his own women.

He felt the impact and Jibril's head snapped back. As Jibril staggered backwards, pain streaked up Dakan's arm.

Not good enough. Jibril wasn't on the floor yet. And his hand could handle another round.

Dakan pursued him, fists balling.

Before that satisfying second crunch, something big and heavy impacted him from the side and he landed hard beneath the force of the tackle and the body that landed on top of him.

He twisted, shoving at his attacker. Another Al-Haaken?

No. Zahir.

"What are you doing?" Zahir bit out in a sharp whisper, one hand locking around Dakan's wrist in the same fashion as he'd detained Jibril.

"Fixing something," Dakan bit back.

"Guards!" *Well, damn. Father.* "Detain my younger son." Quietly angry again. The next thing he knew, several hands had him up and were marching him toward a side entrance.

Nira sought Adele at the start of the party, hoping to compare henna designs from the artist who'd shown up at the penthouse yesterday morning, only to find Adele entirely henna-free.

"But this is your wedding celebration. Everything I've read and watched online says you should have these for your wedding. I just thought that you and Leila had yours together and the artist came to the penthouse to find me."

"No, no one came yesterday. Did you have to sit still for hours while it dried?"

"Yes. But I really wanted to have it done sometime. It's so beautiful." She searched the ballroom, hoping to see Dakan. Would he have sent the artist to her? The man had been steadfastly avoiding her, other than the strange spying interlude. This didn't seem like the kind of thoughtful gesture a man who wanted nothing to do with her would make. She didn't even know where to file this memory aside from Sweet, Thoughtful, and Riddled with Mixed Signals.

If he'd sent the henna artist, it meant he remembered her very first tirade about how all she knew she'd learned online.

It meant he'd been thinking of her—which was at least something.

A man shouted, "Whore's son," and her thought train was derailed amid a ballroom full of gasps. She turned in time to see Zahir and Dakan go flying. Before she could even form the intention to approach them Dakan was marched out by guards.

The march took them directly past her, and Nira's heart banged out of rhythm as his dark eyes again met her own. He shook his head minutely and glanced back toward the rude man. What did that mean?

Leila fluttered toward the man Dakan had hit, ready to usher him out of the room. Damage control, no doubt. That's when she got a good look at him.

"Nira?"

Adele said her name, grabbing her arm. "You've gone as white as a sheet. Let's sit down."

She trailed where Adele led and sat like a sack

of potatoes. Music that had gone quiet at some point resumed, and people began to mingle again.

"He shook his head at me," Nira said, looking at Adele. "Don't go over there. Don't speak to that man. I think that's what he meant."

"Well, that man was shouting very rude things," Adele began, but clearly didn't know the context.

She watched the door Leila and the man had passed through. "I think he's my father."

Dakan had punched her father in the face. After having been called a whore's son.

"Do you think he was calling the Queen that?"

"If he had been, Zahir would've leapt on him, not Dakan. He's the Prince you were telling me about?"

Nira nodded. It was him. He'd aged very well, although it was now possible he'd return home with a different-shaped nose...

"Was he the one who had tried to marry Leila?" Adele asked.

"That was his king." She'd learned only enough of that to know there was a story: two men who had wanted the same woman and a rivalry birthed by the one who'd not been selected. "Dakan hit him. I think he hit him for me." She wanted to go and find where they'd dragged him off to but she wasn't family. "I think he meant my mum."

Adele motioned for a waiter, and soon a glass of juice was placed before Nira. "Drink this. You're still very pale."

Nira dutifully picked up the glass, as she'd been told. Her hand shook and the liquid sloshed about enough that she had to add her other hand to the glass to steady it enough to get to her mouth, and split her attention between drinking and answering Adele's questions about her blood sugar.

Had he sent her mother away? Maybe she'd seen this side of him and had left on her own. Maybe that was where his venom came from.

How dared he call her mum that vile word when he had been *married* while dallying with her?

Leila came back without Jibril, and straight back out the door Daken had been escorted through.

Adele came back and placed a plate with some nuts, fruit, and cheese on it in front of her. "Eat these."

"Will you take me to where Dakan is?" Nira wasn't interested in food.

"Not until you eat something."

All this being bossed around was getting really old. But Nira plucked up to cubes of cheese and popped them into her mouth, which turned out to be a lot of cheese to chew at once.

"Finish that small plate and then I'll take you."

"Every time I come here, I try to be what is expected of me. This was too important for me to just let someone else deal with it. I handled it as well as I could," Dakan said, his head now hurting almost as much as his hand. "Frankly, he needed a hell of a lot more than one punch."

"You try to be what's expected of you?" Mother repeated. "You usually aren't angry like this, so your cheek can be endearing. But when you turn violent toward a guest..."

"A guest who was invited why? You knew who he was. You knew *how* he was." Dakan shifted his attention to his father. "Who were you trying to provoke by inviting him? King Ahmad? Or me?"

"I wanted to confirm the link to Nira's mother," the King said. "It matters to her future and to yours. One of these days you will come to realize you wish to be with her, and that will not happen if she's in Tabda Aljann. But here, in Mamlakat Almas, we have the advantage."

"I'm not going to marry Nira." How many times did he have to say it?

"Why?" His long-silent brother finally broke in. "You love her. You don't deny you love her, you provoke international incidents because you love her, but you don't speak to her, you don't look at her. What is it you do wish from her?"

Dakan had been asking himself the same thing for weeks. He wanted to be with her, and he wanted to protect her, but it didn't feel like a right that belonged to him, even though he knew his aversion to the idea of marriage wasn't entirely rational. He couldn't even understand it himself, it was just there, part of a future that didn't feel like it belonged to him.

"I don't think I'd be a good husband, and likely a worse father—she's had enough experience with those. As you've said, I've a number of character defects. It's better she finds that out before children get involved."

"Ridiculous," Zahir said. "And that still doesn't explain why you attacked Jibril. Tell us. What were you thinking?" It'd been years since he'd angered his brother enough to cause his spine to go rigid and that tone come to his voice. Zahir's disappointment bothered him more than their parents', but mostly what he felt in that moment was apathy for the entire situation. The fire that had blazed was…depleted.

"How about I just go to my suite and you all return to the party?" Which his little showdown with Jibril had interrupted. "I *am* sorry for disrupting your celebration."

"You're not forgiven," Zahir said hotly. "Name a reason. Give us something we can use to smooth this over without an explanation that would shame Nira and her mother publicly. Otherwise it will be time for grand gestures. If that punch was your way of telling her you love her because you're not man enough to say it directly, I don't know what we can do with you."

Dakan said the only thing he could—the truth. "I wanted to spare Nira further humiliation at the hands of Jibril after…"

"After what?"

"After I did to Nira what Jibril did to her mother." Dakan stood to face what must come. He knew what grand gestures meant: justice to the victim. Punishment.

"She's pregnant?" Fatiq asked.

"No. But I took her to bed knowing we'd never be what she wanted. When he called her mother a whore, I heard his words extending to Nira and saw red." Dakan drew a deep breath. He had no idea what else to say.

The door opened to the ballroom and Nira and Adele stepped through. He looked at her long enough to decide she hadn't been crying, so maybe Jibril had stayed away or left—the only positive he could take away from the evening.

Turning back to his family, he muttered, "I have no other explanations. Do what you will. Make your grand gesture."

"Grand gesture?" Nira's voice came from behind him, alarmed, but he didn't turn back, just waited for the pronouncement.

"Very well," Father said, his voice resigned, like he'd always expected things with Dakan to come to this. "Can Zahir continue the work you began from England?"

"It's all lined out in proposals. I've hired an agent here to organize the budgets and another..." Dakan stopped. He wasn't asking for details. "I have meticulous notes and two agents to help. They're very efficient. It can all be managed by phone or email."

Just get on with it.

This wasn't how he'd intended to get back to London, but it would serve. He'd have to hope

Nira would reach the same point soon and return home to finish the plans. Maybe his sentence would provide initiative.

"Dakan Al Rahal, for breaching the sacred duty of hospitality and attacking our guest, you are exiled to the desert."

Dakan stilled. Those weren't the words he'd expected. A dressing down for improper behavior, yes, not a reminder that he'd violated ancient, even holy ways.

"Your passport is revoked. You will not leave our kingdom. You will not enter our cities. Until you can produce answers, you will not become a guest in another country, and you are no longer a prince of your own."

Nira's throat went as dry as that desert they were sending him into. What did banishment to the desert even mean? Was it a death sentence?

"Fatiq, that's too harsh," Leila said, stepping closer to Dakan.

Dakan put his arm around her shoulders and murmured something at her temple. Whatever he said, Nira could see the tension in his frame. Stiff Dakan, Prince Dakan. Not himself. Was he ever himself with them? She hadn't ever seen him do anything but argue with his father.

"The desert always has answers," Zahir said. "Meditate. Ask for guidance. I know you've never believed in it, but do it anyway."

"At least confine him until first light." Leila was the only other person in the room who seemed as bothered by this as Nira was. "He shouldn't travel in the desert at night."

The King nodded.

First light meant travel under the brutal sun. How was that better?

Dakan kissed the Queen's cheek, then turned and walked straight toward Nira.

Weeks with no contact, but simply seeing him walk toward her with that purposeful stride and determined glint in his dark eyes sent her still smoldering spark into a conflagration.

He didn't stop until he was chest to chest with her, his hands on her cheeks and his mouth sealed to hers. The kiss was so bare and pained, she felt drenched by it. He kissed her like a man who would never know pleasure or peace again.

Nira curled her hands into the lapels of his tux, keeping him there, taking all the feeling pouring through his kiss.

"Don't wait for me," he said against her lips when they both came up for air—exactly the opposite from what his kiss had said to her. "Go home. Be happy."

Other people pulled him from her. Once again, guards marched him away before she could think of a single thing to say that might make the situation better. Right after he'd told her not to wait for him seemed like the wrong time for a declaration of love.

As they approached a large archway on the other side of the atrium, he called over his shoulder in English, "Don't go near him, Nira. Don't talk to him. Don't go to Tabda Aljann. Don't go to him, do you hear me?" As they rounded the corner of the arch he met her gaze again and dug his feet in to make them pause.

Another story she didn't know about her father. The difference was that this time she'd seen enough to make the leap of faith. Between Mum's reaction to Jibril and Dakan's, all her questions had been effectively answered.

"I won't," she answered, saying the words he needed, though she probably would've agreed even if she hadn't meant it at that point.

He smiled, a subdued version of that grin that always made her heart melt, and then he was gone.

Tears threatened, but Nira wasn't about to cry

in front of the King, who had banished him. For her, the party was over, but no excuses came to mind for her to make. She just curtsied, gathered the skirts of her expensive gown and muttered, "Please excuse me."

Once through the door, she skirted the ballroom, ignoring the curious looks from guests. Her mind swarmed with too many thoughts to focus on anything except what was essential to her sanity.

Get to the room.

Get her sketchbook.

Let her brain switch off.

CHAPTER FOURTEEN

IT WAS PART of Dakan's make-up to always test boundaries.

He'd been the child who would touch a bee after someone had told him it would sting him, just to see for himself.

Don't eat chocolate before bed or you'll be sick. He ate the chocolate.

Don't come back to the city until you sort yourself out.

Dakan wanted to go back to the city. He wanted to go to the penthouse, wait for Nira to come, and take another bath.

Meditate and ask the desert for answers? He'd fall asleep or die from some wasting sickness before the desert gave him any answers. He didn't even know the stupid question—which seemed the bare minimum to know when starting a quest for answers.

A week in, and out of things to do, Dakan gave in and called Zahir. How did someone seek answers in the desert?

An hour after the call ended, Dakan dressed and readied himself to walk in the desert, still with no idea about the question.

By late afternoon he'd found the grave of his baby brother, and sat there for a while, picturing what life would've been like with three of them and the Lego house at eleven, six and four.

Aafaq would've played inside with him—Zahir had been too old to get excited about the play-house.

He would've been the middle brother. Would that have changed who he was the way Nira believed being kept from her heritage had changed her?

Dakan had never visited Aafaq's grave before, and he'd never meditated either.

Today he did both. A long talk he couldn't finish before he ran out of water and had to return to camp.

Before he'd even quenched his thirst, he knew he'd return the next day.

Zahir and Adele returned to England a week after their celebration, and Nira was tempted to go with them, but she wanted to be there when Dakan came back. The man had failed in his farewell attempt, but he could come back if he came up with whatever answers they wanted, so she waited, worked on the hospital, and walked on the beach with Leila—who was full of informative stories about the Al-Haaken brothers that explained everything she'd witnessed. Information Mum would probably like to know, just as soon as Nira worked out how to bring it up.

She and Adele had exchanged email addresses before they'd gone, and having someone else to talk to made things a little easier. But a half-pound less than unbearable was still a heavy load.

Nothing she did took Dakan from her mind. She didn't even know what he was supposed to be doing in the desert—how could sand tell him anything except that life was hard?

During the weeks since Dakan's exile to the desert, Nira and Leila had spoken daily, though not about Dakan, and because Nira knew it upset the Queen to think of Dakan out there, and because she was the Queen and this whole royalty thing still wigged Nira out a bit, she didn't force the subject. Leila wasn't her Mum, so she needed different tactics from shock and awe.

Into the third week, by the time their midweek beach prowl rolled around, Nira had reached her breaking point. She met Leila and immediately launched in. "I have to say this before I forget how I rehearsed it."

Leila nodded, her expression sharpening with focus.

"I want to go to Dakan, wherever he is. I think he needs someone to talk to. He doesn't like to talk about feelings or even think about them. If he's supposed to meditate and find answers, how is he going to do that when he doesn't even...?" *Hell, how did that part go?* "He doesn't even know himself. Do you know where he is? Can you help me get to him?"

Leila's smile was slow. "His life isn't in much danger there. He has been at our desert abode, he's not suffering as you think he is. At least not physically. Emotionally... Well, when there is nothing left for him to distract himself with, Dakan will listen to that quiet voice in his heart."

"So this is a thing he does?"

Leila shook her head and stepped in to put her arm around Nira's shoulders. "No. My youngest is very like me in that he has a great capacity to creatively amuse or distract himself. But he also has Fatiq's stubbornness."

"So what happens if he doesn't have some kind

of epiphany when he's there? How long does his exile last?"

"It lasts until he can give a satisfactory response for the incident and his handling of this mess. Or perhaps until he simply gives in and does what Fatiq wishes."

"Marry me?"

Leila nodded.

"Oh, that's exactly what a woman wants to hear about her reluctant possible future husband. If it turns out he's the less stubborn of the two and gets bored, he might decide to marry me just so he can have electricity again."

"I don't think that will happen."

"I could help him, Leila. If we're alone, he'll talk to me. I know he will."

"Give him more time." Leila steered her toward the water. They always walked at the water's edge. It was no good to walk on the beach without getting your feet wet and feeling the sand between your toes.

Too much like walking in the desert.

When Nira got to the penthouse the next morning for work, Leila was sitting at her desk, waiting. The first thing that hit her was surprise, then fear.

"Has something happened to Dakan?"

The Queen rose. Behind her chair sat a medium-sized travel bag. "Dakan is fine. I'm here to help you, but only if you agree not to share your decision when I have finished saying what I came to say."

Keep her decision to herself? She could do that. "I agree."

"The day you came to us, Dakan asked me to protect your freedom. Yesterday my first instinct was to protect you physically, then I remembered his request. So here I am."

The conversation was quick, and Leila left as soon as it was over.

Two hours later the helicopter landed on the outside edge of the oasis, letting Nira off with her bag.

A man came out to meet her and Nira handed him an envelope Leila had given her, granting permission to be there.

With nothing to argue about, he gestured to the big tent—as if Nira could miss the thing—and left her to it.

Inside, she found layers of Arabian rugs, pillows for sitting on, cascades of white silk, intricate bronzed lanterns and a fire pit—though she couldn't imagine where wood to burn came from, or even if it was for burning wood.

It was so large there were rooms, separate tents connected together with enclosed passageways leading from one to the next.

In one, a bedroom, there was a massive four-poster bed and a thick velvet rope above it. Okay, that was a little weird.

She went through the whole complex, at least everywhere she could find, and Dakan wasn't there. But the massive bed looked comfortable, so she returned there and climbed up onto it. In the middle, she found an open notebook with an ink pen lying on the open page.

Left to right writing.

English.

She leaned over to peek at it, and the words "Dear Nira" stood out.

A letter to her.

She reached for the book.

As he now did every day, Dakan returned to the camp at dusk. Tonight, one of the groomsmen met him in front of the tent and held an envelope out to him. He found his mother's elegant script on the front, but it wasn't addressed to him. He stepped into the tent and removed his shoes to get a little more comfortable, lit a lantern and opened the envelope.

He hadn't expected to hear from her yet—Dakan knew by now that people watched him, and servants made reports. The family knew he was fine, aside from the headache that hadn't left him since he'd arrived. The one that had stayed so long he'd started to think he had a blasted brain tumor...

What he found inside the envelope sent a thrill through him, and left him feeling a little breathless. Dropping the letter, he picked up the lantern and went deeper into the tent.

Nira had permission to be there.

He found her in the harem room, a lantern hanging nearby and his notebook open in her lap. If she'd read the whole thing, she'd never give up on him, even though she should. But he couldn't think about that now—he was so incredibly grateful to see her...

Her hair was down and she wore loose-fitting trousers and a T-shirt. Little bare feet wedged beneath each knee, she didn't seem to realize he was there.

"Why did you pick the harem room?" he asked,

unable to help the smile that came when she lifted her eyes to him.

"Because I'm not a royal, and this is the royal abode. It seemed like the most appropriate room for me, class-wise."

"I'm not a royal either right now. Perhaps we should both join the harem."

She fidgeted with the corner of one page, nervously flicking it back and forth. "I think we're too well educated for that. Though I have to comment on this book. There are twelve letters addressed to me, their perforated edges still perfectly intact. When were you going to send them? The same day you decided to trim that beard, Wild Man?"

Her tease made him smile again, but his throat felt thick and his tongue sluggish. "I had no one to impress." He cleared his throat and walked fully into the tent to sit on the corner of the pillow-mattress. "I didn't intend to send them to you."

"Then why did you write them?"

"To try and make sense of things. I missed our conversations, so I wrote to you."

"Who is Aafaq?"

Dakan reached for the notebook, but she pulled it out of his reach.

"Aafaq was what they called my little brother. He was born too soon in order to save Mother's life. Zahir told me to talk to the desert, but that's just not me. If I'm going to sit in the desert and talk to anything, it'd be my little brother. His grave's nearby."

There it was again, that compassion in her eyes that felt like a caress.

"Is that where you were today? It can't be too close. The helicopter is loud."

"I heard it. Just decided it was Father, and he could wait. If I'd known it was you, I'd have come right away."

"You would've?" The sadness he'd inflicted on her pulled at her brows, still present even if she was happy to see him, and that light was there too. "You did a good job of avoiding me at the palace. You should know, I took a gamble coming here."

"What gamble?"

"If we don't talk through this and work things out, I'll be sent back to England and the project given to someone else."

Dakan lifted a hand to rub it over his face, and immediately knew how he must look. Dirty. Hairy. Not at all princely. But then, that was who she'd come to see. She didn't like it when he got stiff and princely.

"You shouldn't have come, then."

"It's too late now. If I leave, your people here will report to the palace that I was here. For better or worse, we need to work this out and I think we can."

"You continue to give me too much credit." He lay back on the bed and stared at the ceiling. "I thought you came to talk about your father. Have the Al-Haaken contacted Father?"

"I don't know, and I really don't care unless it's important to you." She scooted to his side, but didn't touch him. "I want to talk about the letters."

"The letters are me trying to explain what I'm thinking after my graveside chats with Aafaq."

She flipped through the pages, though he was certain she'd read it all before he'd returned. "I like the questions at the top of the pages. *How would I be different if Aafaq had lived? Why does it bother me to be labeled 'Born to Follow'?*" She met his gaze, her brow lifted. "That's the first two pages devoted to relationships between brothers."

"Aafaq is my brother. I don't know the question to ask, so I just started the conversations thinking about what it means to be brothers. If I'd been second in line but not the youngest, would I be different? Would I have gravitated more toward Zahir's territory, been more like Prince Dakan—as you dubbed me—without forcing it?"

"Territory. If we were home, I'd make it a drinking game. Every time you said 'Zahir's territory,' you'd have to do a shot."

"Too bad we're not in England."

"If we were, we wouldn't talk. We'd just get drunk and then nakedness would inevitably follow."

Damned right it would. His willpower was shot.

"You frame it as relationships between brothers, but your brothers didn't cast your role. Your parents did that. The King—who I'm sure loves you in his authoritarian way—was the one who said you were born to follow. He probably didn't think about how that would stick with a child. And that would bother anyone, especially someone in your position. If someone told you that you were predetermined for greatness, that'd be a lot easier fate to embrace than being born to do whatever your brother told you. It's not about Zahir, it's about having your free will reined in before you could even understand what it meant."

Dakan really hated thinking about feelings, but

he loved it that she was close enough to him now that he could touch her. She wouldn't let him take the notebook, so he reached for her hand again and let himself soak in the tangible physical relief he felt touching her.

His head instantly stopped aching.

She set the notebook on the bed beside her, freeing her other hand to reach for his. "What's wrong?"

"My head…feels so much better I'm a little light-headed."

He needed her around, even if it was an entirely selfish desire.

"Do you want me to stop?"

He shook his head. She wanted to talk, so he wanted to do whatever she wanted. Even if it was on unpleasant topics, he had missed their talks. He'd missed her voice. Her scent. Everything.

"When you're in London and you see Zahir, do you feel the need to be Prince Dakan?" Her thumbs began stroking his fingers.

"No."

"Then I don't think you're really talking about brother problems. It's not about Zahir. You can let go of that guilt." She momentarily pulled her hand away to flip the notebook pages and read back his words, "'I enjoy working on the hospital. It lets me do something important for my country—which is a new experience for me. I've never been important to the country, or felt I could be without something happening to Zahir, a thought that brings a mountain of guilt.'"

"I know what I wrote," he murmured, catching her free hand again. "Do you know the question?"

"I know the answer," she said softly, smiling in that soothing way.

She knew the answer? "What is it? Tell me and I'll come back."

"No. If I tell you what to think, it's never going to be real for either of us. If you ever decide you can have what we both want, even if you're uncertain about everything else in life, you have to be certain about us. I need you to know it like I know it, deep in your heart."

"If you tell me, I'll believe, *habibi*. I swear."

"I didn't come here to do your thinking for you." She lifted his dry, weathered hands and kissed the thumbs wrapped over her fingers. "I know you can do it. It's all in that notebook. Have you gone back and read it all together?"

"No."

"You should. Even if there's not one mention of

territory in this book. All the times you've mentioned Zahir's territory in conversation points to
it meaning something you haven't explored yet."

"All it means is that I'm better at different things
than he is. I'm not him. If he's better at something,
he should be the one doing it. People shouldn't
expect me to be good at it too just because he is.
We're different."

"Yes, you are. So different it looks contrived,
like all those television shows and movies about
opposites who live or work together, and the
kooky shenanigans that ensue when they try to
get along." She paused and pondered a moment
before announcing, "The things you've said are
Zahir's territory are emergency medicine and mis-
behaving in more satisfying ways, like bombing
your Lego house rather than chopping it up. What
else?"

"Nira."

"No, Nira is pretty much only Dakan's territory,
whether he wants to claim it or not." She suddenly
pulled her hands free of his, and he wanted to grab
her and pull her to him again. "Read the letters
with fresh eyes, as if I'd written them, without all
your preconceived ideas about what you can and
cannot do or what your place is." She leaned to-

wards him and reached down to cup his scruffy cheeks. "And I don't care what answers your family want you to find. I only care about you."

He closed his eyes, nothing coming to him to say other than pleas for her to stay.

"I love you, and I know you love me. I even knew it before I read it. And it's not the kind of love you can walk away from. I've seen up close the effects of twenty-seven years of heartbreak... always bitter and cold and broken. I don't know if he ever truly loved her—I hope he did before it got twisted—but I know she loved him. It never went away."

"Nira...how can I—?"

"Wait. There's one more thing I know. We are supposed to be together. And you're the only thing standing in our way." Her eyes welled up and she lowered her head until her smooth, cool forehead touched his, and her tears fell on the cheeks she held.

She let go and straightened. He couldn't tell whose tears were on his face any more.

"Find me when you're ready," she said, her voice shaking with effort, then turned and walked out of the tent.

Dakan reached for the notebook.

* * *

For the next two days they made love every night, and during the day he went to Aafaq, this time armed with the notebook Nira believed held the answers he needed, but the only questions he cared to have answered were: Why couldn't he have her? Where did this certainty that he couldn't come from?

On the third day he took extra water and food with him to Aafaq's grave, intent on staying until he'd sorted himself out. He had no idea why his father let her stay there without sending the helicopter to retrieve her. He had to sort it out before they took her away from him again, or before she lost faith and left him, even if he longed to spend every minute with her—every minute that twisted together paradise and agony.

Sometime in the middle of the third night Nira felt the bed give beside her and Dakan spooned up behind her. He'd warned before leaving that he wouldn't return until he had an answer, so she'd expected him to be away for days. Her heart immediately launched into a staggering rhythm before he'd even put his arms around her.

"You have answers?" she whispered, then

squirmed around to face him. The lantern she kept lit cast a golden light over his tanned face, and she saw that light in his eyes for the first time in a long time, and the twinkle of mischief she'd so missed.

"You might kick me if I tell you."

"I'll definitely kick you if you don't tell me."

Tugging her beneath him, he rolled her onto her back and sought her mouth. Their kisses were always full of passion, but since that blessed building had swallowed her up they'd been full of love and urgency. The past few days' need had become longing tinged with heartache, and every touch of his lips had broken her heart.

But his kiss now held nothing but love, hope, and promises. He tasted like honey, heady and indolent, like he had all the time in the world.

When he finally lifted his head, she knew the wait was over. It was like peace flowed off him.

"Zahir will be King one day, and the King should always be treated with courtesy and respect," Dakan said softly, combing his fingers through her hair as he held her gaze, staying against her, his face inches away. "It would be disrespectful for me to be better at something than he is, or to even try to be. I'm the one who was born to follow, and I hate it being phrased that way. I didn't—I don't want to just follow. I want to do great things for our people too. So to reconcile those issues, whatever way Zahir went, I went in the other direction. I didn't even realize I was doing it."

Nira nodded, reaching for the buttons down his shirt. The talking would be more fulfilling if she could feel him down the entire length of her body, skin to skin. "Every page in your book led from one piece of the puzzle to the next, did you see it?"

"I saw it," he whispered, pulling the shirt off and helping rid them both of clothes before molding himself back to her.

"How does that explain punching Jibril? Did you work that out?"

"That was me after hitting my snapping point. It started at the penthouse when I defied my father for the first time ever—being directly disrespectful to the king."

"When he told you not to be alone with me?"

He nodded, his arms tightening. The time in the desert had made him a bit leaner, but his appeal was every bit as strong.

"After that, I fought with him on the beach about you. I think at that point I just said to hell with it, and let instinct drive me in matters I couldn't let my prince persona handle diplomatically. I didn't want to leave your future in my father's hands. I don't think he'd hurt you, but I just…couldn't let anyone else take care of you. I wanted it to be me, and it confused me. Plus, let's be real here, Jibril needed punching."

Nira could see the progression, one act of rebellion in a moment of stress, followed by another when the world hadn't imploded the first time. By the time he'd got to Jibril, everything had been so out of control it had probably felt like nothing could make things worse.

Then his words replayed in her mind and she asked, "You fought with the King a second time about me? This was after I moved to the palace?"

"The same day."

"What about?"

"I accused him of bringing you to the palace as leverage in this never-ending conflict with the Al-Haaken, and then refused to marry you. Not that I feel that way now."

"So the King had been trying to make you marry me for weeks?"

"You know, opinions formed by six-year-olds rarely work out well for grown men."

"You think?"

He grinned, and that dimple she'd so missed pitted his cheek again.

"I missed your dimple."

"I missed everything about you. We didn't even get a chance to laze about in bed that day, did we? The King arrived, it all went to hell, and I... Actually, that's the first day I started to really question what I wanted, because I knew I wanted you, even when I denied it to everyone else. I want you, Nira. I want to be with you, and I don't care where. I want you, and our children. I want to be there for you both, for you all, however many of you all there end up being."

She felt his breath fan her lips seconds before the first soft brush of his. Her mouth opened and he deepened the kiss, his body scorching the length of hers as he slid between her legs and set her on fire.

As they came together, peace fell over Nira with the certainty they'd found all their missing pieces. They'd roughed out the footprint and dug the foundations, and could start building a life, a family, a home...wherever they decided to put it. Solid. Beautiful. And built far too well to fall in a lifetime.

* * * * *

If you missed the first story in the
DESERT PRINCE DOCS *duet*
look out for

SEDUCED BY THE SHEIKH SURGEON
by Carol Marinelli

And if you enjoyed this story, check out
these other great reads from Amalie Berlin

TAMING HOLLYWOOD'S ULTIMATE
PLAYBOY

FALLING FOR HER RELUCTANT SHEIKH

SURGEONS, RIVALS...LOVERS

BREAKING HER NO-DATES RULE

All available now!

MILLS & BOON®
Large Print Medical

March

A Daddy for Her Daughter	Tina Beckett
Reunited with His Runaway Bride	Robin Gianna
Rescued by Dr Rafe	Annie Claydon
Saved by the Single Dad	Annie Claydon
Sizzling Nights with Dr Off-Limits	Janice Lynn
Seven Nights with Her Ex	Louisa Heaton

April

Waking Up to Dr Gorgeous	Emily Forbes
Swept Away by the Seductive Stranger	Amy Andrews
One Kiss in Tokyo...	Scarlet Wilson
The Courage to Love Her Army Doc	Karin Baine
Reawakened by the Surgeon's Touch	Jennifer Taylor
Second Chance with Lord Branscombe	Joanna Neil

May

The Nurse's Christmas Gift	Tina Beckett
The Midwife's Pregnancy Miracle	Kate Hardy
Their First Family Christmas	Alison Roberts
The Nightshift Before Christmas	Annie O'Neil
It Started at Christmas...	Janice Lynn
Unwrapped by the Duke	Amy Ruttan

217 LP 2P P1 Medical

MILLS & BOON®
Large Print Medical

June

White Christmas for the Single Mum	Susanne Hampton
A Royal Baby for Christmas	Scarlet Wilson
Playboy on Her Christmas List	Carol Marinelli
The Army Doc's Baby Bombshell	Sue MacKay
The Doctor's Sleigh Bell Proposal	Susan Carlisle
Christmas with the Single Dad	Louisa Heaton

July

Falling for Her Wounded Hero	Marion Lennox
The Surgeon's Baby Surprise	Charlotte Hawkes
Santiago's Convenient Fiancée	Annie O'Neil
Alejandro's Sexy Secret	Amy Ruttan
The Doctor's Diamond Proposal	Annie Claydon
Weekend with the Best Man	Leah Martyn

August

Their Meant-to-Be Baby	Caroline Anderson
A Mummy for His Baby	Molly Evans
Rafael's One Night Bombshell	Tina Beckett
Dante's Shock Proposal	Amalie Berlin
A Forever Family for the Army Doc	Meredith Webber
The Nurse and the Single Dad	Dianne Drake

MILLS & BOON®
Large Print Medical

March

A Daddy for Her Daughter	Tina Beckett
Reunited with His Runaway Bride	Robin Gianna
Rescued by Dr Rafe	Annie Claydon
Saved by the Single Dad	Annie Claydon
Sizzling Nights with Dr Off-Limits	Janice Lynn
Seven Nights with Her Ex	Louisa Heaton

April

Waking Up to Dr Gorgeous	Emily Forbes
Swept Away by the Seductive Stranger	Amy Andrews
One Kiss in Tokyo...	Scarlet Wilson
The Courage to Love Her Army Doc	Karin Baine
Reawakened by the Surgeon's Touch	Jennifer Taylor
Second Chance with Lord Branscombe	Joanna Neil

May

The Nurse's Christmas Gift	Tina Beckett
The Midwife's Pregnancy Miracle	Kate Hardy
Their First Family Christmas	Alison Roberts
The Nightshift Before Christmas	Annie O'Neil
It Started at Christmas...	Janice Lynn
Unwrapped by the Duke	Amy Ruttan

MILLS & BOON®
Large Print Medical

June

White Christmas for the Single Mum	Susanne Hampton
A Royal Baby for Christmas	Scarlet Wilson
Playboy on Her Christmas List	Carol Marinelli
The Army Doc's Baby Bombshell	Sue MacKay
The Doctor's Sleigh Bell Proposal	Susan Carlisle
Christmas with the Single Dad	Louisa Heaton

July

Falling for Her Wounded Hero	Marion Lennox
The Surgeon's Baby Surprise	Charlotte Hawkes
Santiago's Convenient Fiancée	Annie O'Neil
Alejandro's Sexy Secret	Amy Ruttan
The Doctor's Diamond Proposal	Annie Claydon
Weekend with the Best Man	Leah Martyn

August

Their Meant-to-Be Baby	Caroline Anderson
A Mummy for His Baby	Molly Evans
Rafael's One Night Bombshell	Tina Beckett
Dante's Shock Proposal	Amalie Berlin
A Forever Family for the Army Doc	Meredith Webber
The Nurse and the Single Dad	Dianne Drake

MILLS & BOON®
Large Print – March 2017

ROMANCE

Di Sione's Virgin Mistress	Sharon Kendrick
Snowbound with His Innocent Temptation	Cathy Williams
The Italian's Christmas Child	Lynne Graham
A Diamond for Del Rio's Housekeeper	Susan Stephens
Claiming His Christmas Consequence	Michelle Smart
One Night with Gael	Maya Blake
Married for the Italian's Heir	Rachael Thomas
Christmas Baby for the Princess	Barbara Wallace
Greek Tycoon's Mistletoe Proposal	Kandy Shepherd
The Billionaire's Prize	Rebecca Winters
The Earl's Snow-Kissed Proposal	Nina Milne

HISTORICAL

The Runaway Governess	Liz Tyner
The Winterley Scandal	Elizabeth Beacon
The Queen's Christmas Summons	Amanda McCabe
The Discerning Gentleman's Guide	Virginia Heath

MEDICAL

A Daddy for Her Daughter	Tina Beckett
Reunited with His Runaway Bride	Robin Gianna
Rescued by Dr Rafe	Annie Claydon
Saved by the Single Dad	Annie Claydon
Sizzling Nights with Dr Off-Limits	Janice Lynn
Seven Nights with Her Ex	Louisa Heaton

0217 GEN STD LP

MILLS & BOON®

Why shop at millsandboon.co.uk?

Each year, thousands of romance readers find their perfect read at millsandboon.co.uk. That's because we're passionate about bringing you the very best romantic fiction. Here are some of the advantages of shopping at www.millsandboon.co.uk:

* **Get new books first**—you'll be able to buy your favourite books one month before they hit the shops

* **Get exclusive discounts**—you'll also be able to buy our specially created monthly collections, with up to 50% off the RRP

* **Find your favourite authors**—latest news, interviews and new releases for all your favourite authors and series on our website, plus ideas for what to try next

* **Join in**—once you've bought your favourite books, don't forget to register with us to rate, review and join in the discussions

Visit **www.millsandboon.co.uk**
for all this and more today!